CHRISTOPHER'S
DILEMMA

Telham Park novels by

Jennifer Burton:

Princess' Journey

Christopher's Dilemma

Kenya's Song

Brian's Connection

Telham Park

CHRISTOPHER'S DILEMMA

JENNIFER BURTON

 ALEXZUS BOOKS

New York

ALEXZUS Books
244 Fifth Avenue
Suite B260
New York, NY 10001

Cover design by Rick Turylo

ISBN 978-0-9724733-3-0

Library of Congress number 2011909032

Printed in the United States of America

February 2012

For Malachi Sean

one

Christopher found Deshon's heavy pounding intrusive, in fact annoying, but there was no distracting him from Matthew Henson's documentary on cable network's *Truth Factor*. Flushed with pride, he raised the volume and eased back on the sofa. "This is for real, yo. Check this out."

Deshon was hammering the finishing nails into a wood cabinet he was building and didn't hear a word his best friend said.

Watching television at five o' clock during a weeknight was unusual for Christopher. Normally, he'd be on his job—cleaning engines, rotating tires, wet sanding or washing down the used cars for sale—at Magic Auto Center. But today he swapped a working day to attend a military recruitment seminar.

Christopher wasn't in the least bit deceived by the uniformed officers' campaign to enlist or the noble picture they painted about fighting—in what he considered to be—an unjust and unnecessary war. Deshon agreed and by 2:45 they were out of there and found their way to Deshon's basement. They indulged themselves in microwave popcorn, turkey burgers with cheese and chips and drank one of Deshon's father's beers.

The irritating pounding suddenly ceased. Examining his work, Deshon ran his fingers around the edges, inspecting the precision of the cabinet's sliding inner grooves. "Yeah . . . that's whassup," he mumbled. Satisfied with the result, he boxed his tools and reached in his pocket to answer his vibrating phone.

"Where y'all at?" he balked, peering intently in the closet mirror. The diamonds inside the gold cross he wore around his neck glistened against his caramel wool sweater, which was a tiny shade lighter than his boots.

Unlike Christopher, Deshon liked to talk, much about nothing; that is, when he wasn't building something. It was decided that his creative hands far outweighed his glib tongue; in fact, they were gifted. He could envision an object, create a prototype, and replicate it to perfection. Once he made a bookshelf from the drawers of an old dresser that a neighbor had thrown away. It was stained in cherry-red mahogany and finished in high-gloss polyurethane. For his parents, Deshon had made a mobile file cabinet out of eighteen-inch wood panels and attached casters to the bottom. Later on he built a working desk to match.

"Forty-five minutes," uttered Christopher, jolted by the factual evidence. "That's a long time."

Deshon was still on the phone. "Ron wit'chu?" he asked, pulling at his oversized jeans hanging below his waist. "Okay, I'm coming right now . . . ight." Approving his appearance, he ran his hand down the back of his smooth Ceasar and passed his Vaseline balm swiftly over his lips.

"Ay, Ron's over there at Doobey's, you wit it?" Deshon asked Christopher, grabbing his coat. "Ayo, ya heard?"

"In forty-five minutes I could be—"

"Nah, that's too long," he objected, picking up the remote control. "I'm talkin' now."

"Leave it alone!" protested Christopher, lifting a hand to halt Deshon's intention. "Listen to this."

"C'mon yo, listen for what?"

" 'Cause you might learn somethin'."

Disinterested, Deshon turned to the wall mirror and inserted the diamond studs in both his ears while appraising his feature-friendly looks—cunning coffee-brown eyes set amid his reddish-brown skin.

"Shoot, I could be in Connecticut in forty-five minutes," said Christopher powering off.

"Yeah, and I could be at Ron's crib lockin' lips with Vanessa. C'mon, we out!"

"That was so wrong," Christopher said, putting on his coat. At six-feet even, he was two inches taller than his friend, darker with a goatee that was growing thicker by the day. "The man reached the top of that mountain, ninety degrees *north*, like forty-five minutes before the rest of them did. He was the one that put the American flag in the earth, where the North Pole is today . . . and they still cut him out the deal."

"Who you talkin' 'bout?"

"Matthew Alexander Henson, son—a Black explorer."

"Who ever heard of a Black—"

"He discovered the North Pole, yo."

"Word?"

"Yeah. First time I'm hearing about him, too. They said he was traveling with this Navy admiral . . . think his name was Peary or Perry, somethin' like that. Anyway, they were searching for the North Pole—him, the admiral, and four other white dudes, for something like . . . eighteen years. Said he couldn't make a journey without him 'cause Henson was everything he needed. The man was strong, a master mechanic . . . oh, and he knew the Eskimo language."

"Uh huh."

"So the admiral told him to go one way, but he went another. Dude said forget this, I've been exploring just like you. So he kept movin' until he got to the top of the mountain. Then, when the others got there, they realized it was the North Pole."

"Serious?"

"Henson had been there for forty-five minutes waiting for everybody else to get there," Christopher explained. "But nobody wanted to give him the credit. C'mon, he was a Black man. And back then, a discovery like that you figure, was like reaching the moon."

Darkness had descended upon the city. Streetlights garishly illuminated the hard-striving area of Brooklyn known as Telham Park. The two boys walked evenly, their strides almost matching as the brisk wind cut across their faces when they turned the corner.

"Okay, so whatchu sayin' is the brother really discovered the North Pole."

"That's right! Technically, he was the first one to get there. It's been documented! I don't understand how they got away without giving the man his credit. At least recognize the man as co-founder or somethin'. That's what the story was sayin'. Until that Black professor from Harvard brought it out, it was just another lie covered up, like Thomas Jefferson's Black children. And if I didn't catch that piece, I wouldn't have known either. 'Cause what are the chances of us reading about this in school?"

"When Tupac and Biggie come back alive."

"You know what it is, and check it. Now, what . . . almost a hundred years later they're givin' Matthew Henson the Hubbard Medal from the National Geographic Society. The man is long gone. And when he died they buried him in Woodlawn Cemetery with the poor common people. Now, the admiral was buried as a hero in Arlington National Cemetery with all the white, military elite. So the professor protested that, too. Then Clinton came through. He granted the professor's petition to have Henson and his wife interred in Arlington."

"Interred," Deshon muttered thoughtfully. "What's that?"

"That means they moved him out of where he was originally buried, and put him somewhere else."

"That's deep," said Deshon, shaking his head contemptuously.

"They still on this backwardness, yo. Tryin' to keep us out of the loop."

"Yeah, but nothin' stays buried forever. That's what Chaziz is rappin' about . . . truth resurrects."

"Always," agreed Christopher. "That's why you got to be up on your history. You be thinkin' things are one way, making moves based on this premise or that one and come to find out, it's a lie."

"You right."

A new discovery in Black history was more than a moment of enlightenment for Christopher. It filled a void in him left by his father's premature departure. When he was alive they had been a complete family unit and all his accumulated knowledge of history was fed to him from the time he was able to read. As the years went on, Christopher's fetish flourished and he had begun to research and learn on his own what he knew his father would have taught him, had he not died.

Entering the boulevard, an old school jam burst out loudly, dividing their thoughts. Moving in time to the rhythm, they passed through a trail of fragrant oils and alluring incense burning by the Muslim street vendors. Stimulating Deshon's senses—and his overactive libido—he acknowledged the berry-brown cutie ambling toward him with hungry eyes.

"You real sexy Ma, word," he said and she swept past him. "Oh, so now you want to act like you don't know me—"

"That's Shannequa's cousin," said Christopher grabbing him. "She's only thirteen."

"What!" Deshon did a double take. "You see the size of her—"

"Close your mouth and cross the street. I want to see if that book came in yet."

Christopher appreciated the quiet in the Telham Park Book Mart after coming out of the noisy street. Soon he found Elias, the manager, behind the counter. He was a middle-aged white man, slightly graying along the temples, wearing gold-rimmed half-glasses.

"W.E.B. Dubois, right?"

"You remembered."

Elias was impressed by Christopher's interest in history and had always welcomed the challenge of finding books that he requested. "I'm afraid it's not in yet, buddy," he informed Christopher shaking his hand. "Try me next Thursday on that. Oh, but did you get a chance to look at the new series, 'Africa to America, the Journey?' "

"Nah. Who did the research?" Christopher asked, pulled into Elias's question like a magnet.

"Hmm . . . it's a team of historians I believe. Come with me, I'll show you."

"Look at Austin!" screeched a young lady, among the group hanging over the neighborhood newspaper, *The Telham Park Ledger*, distracting Christopher's reading.

"He's not fast enough to carry the team," remarked a guy named James, reading the dismal results of Telham Park High School Track Team in the past weekend's relay competition.

A pang of guilt struck Christopher, knowing the track team's record would read differently with his phenomenal quickness. 'Lightning,' they called him, a nickname that followed him since he was a child. He had been given the name simply because he could outrun all his friends—effortlessly! But running competitively required a regimented, disciplined lifestyle that he wasn't ready to commit to. He had better things on his agenda—so he thought.

Deshon was in the young adult fiction section with a book in his hand, talking to a brown skinned beauty. She was large and big-boned with a strikingly pretty face. Christopher waited through his friend's pretense of interest in books and watched him talk his way into getting her cell phone number.

"Big girls need lovin' too," said Deshon as they exited through the revolving doors. "Ay, how much money you got?" he asked Christopher outside.

"Couple of nickels."

"With your nickels and my pennies, we don't have much."

"You busted again?" Christopher asked. "You need to start sellin' some of them projects you finished, yo . . . make some real dough."

"Why should I do that when I got you workin' for me? Come on, give it up. I'ma stop off at the store."

Christopher swung out his fist sideways and hit Deshon in the center of his chest.

He heaved and wobbled, feigning injury. "It ain't that bad, yo. I already told you. I'ma be takin' care of you one of these days."

"Picture that," Christopher chuckled, entering Boulevard Deli.

"Let me get two loosies," Deshon asked the owner."

"That should have been me," said Christopher, pointing to the notice announcing a $10,000 lottery winner. "First thing I would do, yo—"

Three of them together! Catching the back view of the men who entered the store and dispersed in different directions put Christopher on instant alert. He knew that broad build anywhere and the signature white bandana underneath his cap. It was Big Mo and two other members from the Eastern Thugs. The notorious gang members were responsible for a number of recent crimes, including the death of a young whom he had known for years.

"Let's get out of here," Christopher said.

"Yeah, I forgot. You don't want to get home late and feel the wrath of your moms. She ain't no joke!"

Christopher forced a chuckle at the truth, though that wasn't his concern at the moment. Exiting the deli, Alex and Rahkim flew past them and honked the horn driving a 5 series BMW with Silver Star rims sparkling like shiny silver dollars blasting their radio. After finishing high school only a year ago, they'd landed a record deal for their jazz and rap concept.

"Boyz is cruisin'!" Christopher said.

"That's gonna be me when I start gettin' paid."

"Paid for *what*?"

Deshon stopped suddenly. "Act like you got amnesia if you want to, but my skills is untouchable, yo. Wait till I come out wid it." He began snapping his fingers as he walked. Then he pretended his right fist was an imaginary microphone and tossed his other hand in the air to the groove of his words.

"Listen up y'all, this is how I get down
When my people, look at me, they see Mahogany Gold
'Cause I'm smooth, I got charm, I got a mind, with
some goals
When I speak, people listen, got a tongue so profound
Words so incredible, their edible, no limits, no bounds
Call me witty, call me pretty I can show and can prove
With the gift of my hands—I make my own rules—"

"Okay, okay, you flowin', soundin' good, but you need to throw some history up in there, and some politics to set it off."

"Yeah, put that premium on it," he agreed, lighting his cigarette.

A Yukon Denali stopped at the red light as they crossed. "Yeah, that's what I'ma be ridin' right there. Have all my hunnies sittin' in the back."

"Givin' it all right back to where it came from," Christopher said.

Deshon turned abruptly, uncomfortable with the comment. "That's what you makin' it for, to spend it."

"It's not about spendin' every dime you make, yo. Gotta save, gotta build."

"How you know they're not workin' on gettin' a studio or somethin'?"

Christopher released an exasperated sigh looking into the faces that rushed past him. "Just what we need . . . another studio, so we can turn out more bling-blinging rappaz. The world is turnin' and we standin' still."

"Why you hatin'?" Deshon accused testily.

"Hatin'? C'mon, man. We've been rappin' since the beginning of time. Take it back to the days in West Africa. The flow of the words, that fluency, yo, that can be traced back to the griots. But we got the attention of the world now, so let's say somethin' . . . somethin' that's gonna make a difference. I mean I'm happy for the brothers gettin' paid and all that. Ay . . . wish it was me, but it's time to start turnin' some of them dollars into some real sense."

"Everybody ain't tryin' to be a scholar," Deshon quibbled.

"Yeah, and that's the problem."

"Whatchu talkin'— They're not hustlin' for peanuts or working fast food gigs. They carryin' fat rolls."

"And doing what with it? Ay, you can build an empire workin' that fast food joint. I'ma tell you why. 'Cause a man workin' a burger gig can be hungry . . . and not for food either. He'll work, he'll save, he'll buy or build his own burger joint and leave a legacy to his family, yo. Look at Madam C. J. Walker, Johnson Publications, look at Reginald Lewis and that other Johnson, who started BET. You can't build an empire on rap lyrics. Ain't no legacy in that."

"But they makin' crazy money, son. Look at Pu-Gee and all of them."

"Money is paper, a fleeting thing. You got it today. You givin' it back tomorrow. And down the road, you'll be fryin' fish or moppin' floors."

Deshon feigned a laugh. Christopher was in another league intellectually and he knew he couldn't debate his reasoning. "Here," he said, handing over the cigarette. "I'm breakin' out. You comin' to Doobey's?"

Christopher was tempted to hang out. He stalled at the curb of the boulevard with some impromptu small talk, observing the cars racing by so fast they whistled. Before he could inhale a third time, he began to feel lightheaded. Smoking wasn't a comfortable sport for him; it had just become a little social habit.

"Forget it, yo. I'm out here, so let's go."

Doobey lived around the corner from the game room they were approaching, and almost simultaneously a guy named Tevon pulled up in a silver Lexus with his girl, an explosion of thumping bass announcing their arrival. Rob and another girl sat in the back.

"Whas poppin'?" Deshon said rushing over to the car.

"What you up to?" Rob asked coolly, his arm leaning out of the window. His gold watch, encrusted with diamonds, gleamed from a distance.

"Where you been?" a soft voice asked Christopher from behind.

"Tamika, whatchu doin' out here?"

"Hangin'."

"It's like that, huh?"

"Got all the time you need to get to know me," she said, running her tongue over her bottom lip. She was sensuous and lovely, dark and sexy—but Christopher didn't care for aggressive girls who offered themselves to him on a platter. He remembered his father's words that warned, 'If it's free and easy, you'll pay a high price.'

"A young lady should be more careful 'cause strange things come out at night around here."

"What's that supposed to mean?" she asked coyly.

"Think about it," he told her, then turned toward Deshon. "Meet me inside, yo."

The lighting was dim in the arcade as he entered unacknowledged. The stench of musky bodies hung in the air just beneath the stale odor of cigarettes. Smoking wasn't permitted, but all kind of activities went on there anyway.

Christopher walked to the far end of the open space and into a smaller room where he found a free machine. Under the spell of the tower defense game, time quickly ticked away. Relentless enemies met their demise at the continuous stream of bullets coming hard and fast from a tank that knew no opposition. Defeat didn't exist in Christopher's competitive mode. Using his special powers, he dodged every situation leaving no opportunities to damage the tower. It was still standing when he looked around and found himself surprisingly alone. He checked his watch reading 6:21 and dashed out.

Streaks of colorful lights flashed over the walls of the abandoned front room, the lulling sound of the pinball machinery echoing. Outside, the Lexus was sandwiched between two police cars, and there was an eerie quiet given the large number of people standing around.

"What happened?" Christopher called out to anyone who was willing to answer.

"Dudes in a Jeep rolled up on the Lexus and started fightin'," a young man replied. "Then somebody started shootin'."

"Anybody got hit?" Christopher questioned desperately, looking for Deshon.

"Nah. They were lucky," someone said. "But one of the bullets busted out the back window."

"I think that dude over there got sliced," said an older gentleman.

Tevon and Rob were standing outside the Lexus and there was shattered glass all over the ground. In the police car behind him sat two men in handcuffs. Christopher recognized the taller one from the Eastern Thugs; he was a skilled car thief. He strode toward Tevon and Rob when he saw Deshon sitting in the back seat of the other patrol car with a towel wrapped around his arm, his face wracked in agony. In that instant the crowd dispersed as paramedics moved in. There was nothing Christopher could do as he saw his friend being helped into the ambulance and rushed to the hospital.

Christopher couldn't get home soon enough. Flashbacks of the drama unnerved him as he imagined being in that car, getting arrested, and having some police official call his house and tell his mother that he had joined the ranks of Black youth offenders. The words she'd repeatedly spoken rang out in his head: "If the police ever call me and tell me you've been locked up, get comfortable, because I'm not rescuing any criminals."

A three-quarter moon was visible in the dark sky. The decreasing temperature brought on a hair-raising chill in the air. When Christopher glanced through the window of the Spanish bodega, and the big clock read fourteen minutes before seven, he picked up his pace.

"Chris! Chris!" He heard someone calling as he cut between the cars on the boulevard. Ty Davis's husky voice was highly distinguishable.

Christopher turned around, and hurried over to the black Navigator.

"You alright?"

"I'm good," Christopher answered, breathing hard. "I gotta pick up Joshua at Lou Lou's and I'm runnin' late."

"I'll drop you off, c'mon."

It always smelled like fresh pine inside Ty's sport utility vehicle and the music played just above earshot level.

"Working late?"

"You could say that," Christopher replied easily, careful to disguise his troubling thoughts.

Everyone in Telham Park revered Ty—short for Tyrone. At six-foot-three-and-a-half and two-hundred-and-sixty pounds, the golden-brown, bald headed man was a force to be reckoned with. Fearing nothing, the entrepreneur and mentor had a reputation for settling things. And he was as kind as he was brave. He carried grocery bags for elderly ladies, gave women with children rides in inclement weather, and worked soup kitchens during the holidays.

"How you makin' out in school?" Ty asked.

"Doin' alright."

"Alright's not good. What's the problem?"

"Nothing, really. Just not into it."

"Then what's occupying your mind . . . and your time?"

Christopher rubbed his thigh nervously in search of a response. "You know I'm workin' . . . into my history—"

"And what's it teaching you?"

"Lotta things . . . like the truth. I'm not talkin' about that corny version I'm gettin' in school."

"Then you should be learning from others how to plot your direction . . . because now's the time. Don't wait till you get out there and start tripping and stumbling."

Christopher had heard Ty's canned spiel on education dozens of times. "It's essential to a man's well being," he would say. "And if you really wanna be on top of your game, get a law degree. It's always good to know your legal boundaries, especially when you're negotiating." Interestingly, Ty had not always been a sterling role model. He came by his knowledge the hard way—while doing a five-year sentence for manslaughter and possession of a weapon.

Ty grew up poor in Bedville, just south of Telham Park. He was the youngest of eight children born of Southern migrant parents. At age nine, on a snowy January night, when his mother was laboring over dinner, cutting up a chicken into ten pieces to make it stretch, the news came. Ty's father was dead following a sudden heart attack.

The pain wrecked him and he soon turned to gangs as his new family. An articulate and profound storyteller, Ty took you there when he told his story. And just when you were caught up in his adventurous biography, living the dangerous street life, terrorizing gang rivals, dodging bullets and running from the police, he would zap fear into you with the sadistic cruelty and harsh reality of prison.

Reading, Ty soon learned, was the only advantage in serving time. Voracious in his pursuit of knowledge, he would read sometimes fifteen hours a day. He journeyed from ancient to modern literature, examined human distribution through geography, humbled himself through the study of world religions, and sojourned the paths of his ancestry through history.

At the time of his release, Ty Davis walked out of the prison with a bachelor's degree and twelve hundred and fifty-six dollars he'd saved from working. Educated or not, employers were not kind to convicted felons, especially ones the size of Ty. He worked day and night pumping gas for three years. With no social life and no desire to have one, Ty never spent a bad dollar.

When the property next door to the gas station, an old abandoned diner, went up for bid at the city auction, Ty's offer was accepted. With a loan from his former boss, he turned it into a car wash. Work was slow but steady for two years. Ty said he barely had money to eat at times, especially after the bills and his employees were paid.

Then one day, he said, God gave him a break. It was a sort of a sign of forgiveness for his ugly past. An industrial chemical refinery that had been closed for years reopened. A mixture of new elements the plant used had released a chemical ash in the air. The harmless pollutant traveled some two miles, raining over Telham Park and depositing a thin white layer of what looked like snow on all the vehicles parked on the streets.

This sent the residents into a frenzy. The company begged the community's pardon by commissioning Ty's Car Wash to clean thousands of vehicles at their expense—a great opportunity for a fledging entrepreneur. Satisfied customers continued to patronize him, and soon Ty's business skyrocketed. Two years later he purchased a brownstone that had gone into foreclosure and turned it into a classy showplace, beautifully furnished and well maintained.

Christopher's father would have been proud of Ty had he still been alive. James Carlton Murphy had taken a special interest in the troubled seventeen-year old, despite his incorrigible behavior. Back then, Ty was out of control.

"A prison sentence is better than a bullet to the brain," James Murphy told him during his first visit. "God is still with you, boy, even in your madness." He visited Ty faithfully twice a month and encouraged him to begin his life anew. They laughed at the hope of working together in their own establishment one day. Unfortunately, and much to Ty's regret, James Murphy passed away while Ty was still in prison.

After returning home, Ty made it his business to look after Christopher and the family. He and Christopher would go out to eat at least once a week, visit the library or play basketball. In fact, it was Ty who thought Christopher was spending too much time in the neighborhood and asked Victor, his friend and the owner of Magic Auto Center, to give Christopher a job where he could learn a vocation while going to school.

Ty's fist came down hard and heavy on Christopher's fist as he stopped in front of the babysitter's house. "You have to do the work, man. It's hard . . . anything worth having is." Just as he took off he yelled, "And stay out of that game room!"

Surprised, Christopher turned back sharply, wondering what Ty knew, but he was gone.

Christopher rapped hard on the door and paced in a circle awaiting an answer. Joshua, his little brother, opened the door with his jacket and backpack in his hand.

"I got 'im Lou Lou," Christopher confirmed, snatching his brother out of the apartment. "See you tomorrow!"

Joshua's cute round face looked serious as he put his hat atop his kinky-curly hair. "What took you so long?" he asked.

Christopher ignored the question and grabbed his brother's backpack and dodged out to the street.

Entering their building, their sneakers squeaked loudly on the freshly waxed hallway floors and they charged up the stairs.

"Who dat?" asked the elderly gentleman who lived on the first floor.

"It's Chris Pop-Pop."

"Yeah, yeah, okay."

Christopher had been checking on Pop-Pop man since his wife had passed away several years earlier.

Gilroy Harker's trumpet wafted through the second floor as they climbed up higher. He was a sixteen-year-old from Jamaica whose family had come to Telham Park only five years before. Music was a calling he received early and he practiced relentlessly every day for hours. The Murphy's appreciated Gilroy's soothing sound; it was like attending a free concert every evening.

Christopher went to work preparing dinner with frenetic intensity. He preheated the oven, turned on the stove's pilot flame and pulled the steamer out of the cabinet. Inside the refrigerator were seasoned steaks with mounds of onions and peppers, and fresh string beans soaking in a bowl. While searching for the potatoes to bake—the microwave would have to do today—his mind kept returning to Deshon.

"What's the matter?" Joshua asked, sensing trouble. He could speak with inflections that sounded so similar to his father's, it sometimes amazed Christopher.

"Nothing. I'm just tryin' to get everything done before Mommy gets home. You did your homework?"

"Not all of it."

"Okay, finish it now."

"I don't understand how to do this. I need help."

Christopher was caught up in some imaginary scenario and didn't hear Joshua's request.

"Can you help me with my math?" Joshua asked.

"Yeah, yeah, whip it out, li'l man." Softly mumbling, he quickly filled in the answers to the multiplication and division problems. "Here, give it to Mommy to sign. I'll show you how to do it later."

Christopher remembered the last time he got caught in a situation he had no business being in. Challenged by some of the neighborhood boys to make some quick money by gambling, he went up to the roof of the Straton Houses, where one of them lived. While Key Lo, Bruce, and some others smoked marijuana and drank quarts of beer, Christopher swept up all their money playing C-Lo. When they heard the police sirens they fled into one of the boy's homes, a guy named Kwame, and waited until the police were gone.

Later on, Kwame's mother came to the house, spilling her guts out about what had happened. Mrs. Murphy didn't ask any questions. She thanked the woman and practically slammed the door in her face, she was so anxious to deal with Christopher. She lunged at him, pounding him repeatedly with a closed fist.

No, Mommy, no!" Joshua yelled.

"You want to be a criminal?" she admonished, grabbing the neckline of his shirt so tight that Christopher felt as if he were choking.

"And then you embarrass me like this! Mrs. Harris has to come to my home to tell me what you're doing in the street!" Her quiet manner was deceiving, and at times like this she could summon up the fury of a tyrant with an unexplainable force in her hand.

"I work too hard," she was heaving and puffing. "And your father did, too. Think you're a man now, huh? Then it's time to find somewhere else to live. There's plenty of room in the streets for those who don't want to follow rules. So go pack your things and get out! You heard me—out!"

Christopher didn't move. His wandering eyes registered disregard for what she was saying, and he showed no emotion.

"You ignoring me?" she asked, as if daring him to answer with anything other than what she wanted to hear.

"I'm not ignoring you. But I don't understand why you—"

Christopher saw broken streaks of white light when his mother backhanded him, and for a second the room began to spin. But Eleanor Murphy was growing more frustrated at the realization that her boy was no longer a child and would only be but so affected by the strike of her hand. So she hit him again and again and again until her eyes turned glossy, filled with pain.

To see his proud mother reduced to tears was more than he could bear. Christopher surrendered to his hurt and released his pressed lips, allowing his tears to flow. It was the worst punishment he could have ever received. For God's sake, he didn't ever want a repeat of that episode.

"Hey, Mom," Christopher greeted, rushing to the door to relieve her of several grocery bags. "Hang up her coat, Josh."

"You didn't get too far with dinner," she said, entering the kitchen. She placed the mail on top of the counter, soaped up her hands under the tap and briskly washed them. Eleanor Murphy was older than most of his friends' parents, but she looked very youthful. The small framed, reddish-brown woman had a gentle way about her. She was neat and orderly, right down to the simple way she wore her long, straight hair gathered up in a bun. "That's alright, baby, I can finish this."

"No, Ma, I got it. You're tired. Sit down and rest." Christopher put away the groceries just like his mother liked them. He realized she had no knowledge of what had occurred this evening, and for that he was grateful. Inside the pile of mail was a photo card from Princess with her beautiful face gleaming. That was his heart. Inside, it read:

How are you, Christopher? What can I say: You are the best! I was so surprised to receive your gift. It really made my week, and trust me, I put it to some good use. Boarding school is a whole new way of life and I'm still in "adjust mode." Pennsylvania's beautiful in the fall. I miss Telham Park so much and can't wait to come home for the Masquerade party at McCuller's. So much is happening here, I can't wait to tell you. I'll speak with you soon.

Much Love,

Buttah

two

"You got some magical powers or something?" Jordan Nichols said, craning his neck to see what Christopher was reading. There was nothing average about the well-dressed, no-nonsense orator that worked out like a professional body builder. He was one of those smart, committed students at Telham Park High School, and the leading member of the debate team *a.k.a.* Telham Intelligence.

Despite Christopher's efforts to remain aloof in study period by sitting in the back corner of the library, he had been frequently approached. "What's your problem, man? Why you bothering me?"

"I never see you studying, yo . . . and you pass all your tests."

"Don't really have to study. History is truth. Math is logic."

"Logic to you, maybe. That's analytical, right-sided thinking. Me, I'm more intuitive. Rather be doing some research."

"You're poking and prying with some purpose then," Christopher remarked, looking over at the debate team nervously chattering.

"That's what I'm talkin' about, yo. We need you representin'."

Christopher averted his eyes, looking annoyed.

"Think about it," Jordan reasoned. "With you, Telham Intelligence could take Jackson, Hillmore and Beachton."

"Yeah, okay."

"C'mon, we got it all worked out," Jordan persisted, handing Christopher a flyer. "Look." Jordan was an intense person, fashioning his appearance after Malcolm X— the haircut and the glasses too—and ironically, his features were even similar to Malcolm's.

Christopher wasn't moved in the least. What had happened in the game room was still foremost on his mind and he was anxious to see his friend. Deshon had been away from school for the last two days. He wasn't allowed any phone calls or visitors, but his father said he would return to school on Monday.

"I can't get into that right now," he told Jordan. "Talk to me later."

AT FIFTH period Christopher anxiously headed to the cafeteria. A short, thin security officer who looked like a student held up the line, checking class schedules. Christopher was annoyed, but soon relieved when he saw Deshon huddled in the far left corner, seated with their friends.

"What up, fam, you alright?" he asked.

Deshon looked different than usual, with a kind of a scowl on his face. There was no joking, no laughter as they moved away from the crowd to talk in private.

"What happened that night?"

"Friction, yo. It was crazy. The Eastern Thugs were following Tevon and he didn't know it. They were looking for Rob."

"Why?"

"You musta forgot. Rob and his brother Jerome been down with the Dark Shadows a long time."

"Yeah, that's right."

"So after you went inside the game room, I got in the car. Thugs rolled up next to us in a Jeep. Joker snatched me out of there and hit me. Yo . . . I hit 'im back. Next thing I know he whipped out his blade and caught me in the arm. Then Rob jumped out and went to work on him. Then these other dudes jumped out the Jeep. We heard shots and it was on."

Massaging his wound, Deshon chuckled nervously. Then he frowned as if he were in pain. "Felt like somebody jabbed fire in my arm, yo. Had to get fourteen stitches." When he peeled back part of his shirt, his arm was securely bandaged with thick gauze from his shoulder on down.

Sympathy flashed in Christopher's eyes.

"Just a superficial wound," Deshon said. "Ay yo . . . I didn't know what had happened at first. When I realized I was cut . . . it set me *off!*" A sullen look returned to Deshon's face. "We were laughing and jokin' one minute and then . . .

next thing I know I'm bleeding and wobbling to the hospital. My pops was beastin' when he got there. Talking about, 'You gonna get enough of those friends you hangin' out with.' "

"But you weren't runnin' with—"

"Can't tell him that. And accordin' to the Eastern Thugs, I'm running with Rob. When the cops found the knife, the one they call Chill-E got arrested. Before they took him, he told Tevon to sleep with one eye open. They comin' for us."

"Us?"

"That's right. And since you and me is boyz, we both wanted. You know how they do."

Anxiety rose from Christopher's stomach to his throat. "So whatchu gonna do?"

"I'ma be ready for 'em, 'cause I'm not gettin' caught out there like that again."

"Whatchu sayin'?"

"I'ma get down with the Shadows if I have to."

"So you thuggin' now?"

Deshon looked oblivious to the charge. "What I'm supposed to do? Go home, tell my father so he can come to school and talk to the principal?" he said sarcastically. "We talkin' the streets now. This ain't *Happy Days*."

That was the end of the discussion as far as Christopher was concerned. For the remainder of the period he ate his lunch while contemplating his friend's words. The thought of Deshon hooking up with a murderous gang was a very unnerving one.

ON A LAZY, gray Thursday afternoon an unexpected early dismissal bell interrupted Christopher's daydreaming in 8th period science class and required all students to exit the school building. Looking for his friends, he meandered through the crowd and soon spotted Jerome, Alonzo and Maverick.

"Where's Deshon?" Christopher asked.

"The Dean's got him," answered Jerome. He was big—tall and bulky—for his age, about the color of rich cocoa.

"Why, what happened?"

"I don't know," said Maverick, a light-brown young man who was equally as tall but slim and easy going. "I saw them taking him out of class sixth period."

"Somethin's up, yo," remarked Alonzo. "They're detaining him for a reason." The son of a Spanish mother and an Italian father was the color of ivory and his dark eyebrows, thin mustache and shoulder-length hair that he wore in two braids were jet black. The medium-built sophomore had the heart of a lion. And though his real name was Alonzo, everyone called him Al.

"Let's move away from the building," commanded one of the police officers working the crowd.

"And look at all these cops out here," Jerome added. He looked off into the opposite direction of the street and said, "I got my eyes on that blue Jeep. I seen them dudes before, yo. They're Thugs."

"And they lookin' over here," said Alonzo.

"C'mon, let's go," urged Jerome.

"What about Deshon?" Christopher asked as they began to walk.

"He'll be all right," replied Maverick. "They'll probably escort him home or have his father pick him up. But right now, we need to break out of here."

They moved with the crowd, fled down the avenue and then soon parted. With a few more blocks to go before Christopher reached his job, he realized a cobalt blue Jeep Cherokee was trailing behind him. He shifted into high speed and took off running. He cut through a mini-mall and ran behind the parking lot of Evelyn's Southern Fried Chicken, which led to an abandoned area. Before he could get to the main avenue, the Jeep rolled up to the curb, catching him head-on. Three young men jumped out. Two had on leather jackets and one was wearing army fatigues.

"You in a hurry?" the tall, meanest-looking one questioned in a gruff voice. He was wearing a doo-rag and dark glasses.

"Where you goin'?" A second one asked. He was a short, chunkily built, medium-brown-skinned guy with shoulder-length dreadlocks.

Christopher didn't answer, eyeing them suspiciously.

"You alright, man?" the tall one asked. The other two started laughing.

"I'm cool," Christopher replied, his heart pounding so hard he felt as if he were moving when he was really standing still. The volume of the music in the Jeep suddenly quieted, so Christopher knew there was a fourth Thug inside.

"You fight like you run?" the third one asked. His red eyes looked wild and hideous. The scar on his upper right cheek, shaped like a mountain, looked like it could have been a birthmark.

"Nah," Christopher said, shaking his head. "That's not my thing."

"We think it is," the tall one said.

Christopher felt numb with fear, standing alone among the Eastern Thugs. He tried to move around them in quick, deliberate steps.

"You nervous or somethin'?" the chunky one asked. Stepping in tandem, they positioned themselves evenly around Christopher. "Ain't nothin' to be getting' edgy about. We just talkin'."

"But not here like this," the taller one added. "We have something else in mind."

"Nnn . . . no, can't do it today. I'm going to work and I'm runnin' late."

When Christopher attempted to move around them, he was cut off by the third, mean-looking one. "Won't you take a ride with us, yo?"

Christopher wished he could see the tall Thug's eyes through his dark glasses.

"Jerome is your boy, right? I saw you with 'im."

"Let's break out, yo!" a voice yelled out of the Jeep.

In an instant two of them gripped Christopher's arms from behind, startling him. He wrestled himself away but got caught in the clenches of the tall Thug, who slammed his body against the cement wall. Christopher tried to run, but the dark one tackled him. An iron punch to the lower back weakened him. His mother's eyes flashed before him in quick consecutive shots. *How would she react to his bloodied, swollen face and broken ribs—or even the unthinkable? How would she make it if something happened to him? And Joshua?* Fathoming the possibilities, Christopher became relentless, punching with vicious force wherever he could. It was going to be a fight to the bitter end because he was not getting in that Jeep.

One of the Thugs caught him from the back and grabbed his arms. It might have been two, he wasn't sure. That's when the severe punches came. Unable to withstand the force, he groaned heavily, hoping to gain some sympathy.

"Easy, man," he soon heard one of them say.

Christopher was now relieved of the punishing blows and released from their vise-like grips. He was almost afraid to look up, dreading the thought of what was to come.

"Boys' afternoon out?" The hawk-like voice sounded familiar. In a hooded sweat suit and a biker's leather jacket stood Ty, looking large and menacing.

"Just straightening some things out," the tall one said, backing away.

"Any damage?" asked Ty, examining Christopher's face, turning it from side to side.

"Nah, I'm cool."

The strong postures of the Thugs weakened right before their eyes and they made quick tracks to their Jeep. Never taking his eyes off of them, Ty directed Christopher toward his Navigator.

No doubt Ty was a scary force, but he could be mysterious, too. Some of Ty's peers called him "One-Punch Ty" because he once broke a man's jaw and knocked him out cold with just one blow. But even if you didn't know of his boxing prowess, he looked so intimidating that any sane person would proceed with caution.

When Christopher settled inside the Navigator, Ty looked at him closely, concern etched in his face. "You alright?"

"Yeah."

Ty took off fast as if he were in pursuit of someone. "What happened?"

"They came to the school looking for Jerome," Christopher began, passing his hand over his forehead, feeling for any knots or bruises. "Said they saw me with him and wanted to ask some questions."

"About what?"

"Some nonsense, I don't know. But then they wanted me to get in the Jeep. That's when we started fightin'."

Ty could see Christopher slyly examining his still-trembling hands. "They didn't hurt anything, did they?"

"Nah, man . . . nothing I couldn't handle." Christopher replied defensively, well knowing he was lying.

"Stay away from them. You don't want to get involved with that."

"You know I don't roll with them."

"Yeah, but they want you. It's how they start the recruitment process."

Christopher turned his aching head toward Ty. "How you know?"

"I remember those days like it was yesterday, man. Been there and done that. They're trying to strengthen those numbers 'cause the Dark Shadows are slammin' on 'em. They've been watching you."

"For what?"

"Because you're not attached to anything, just bending with the wind. That's the kind of brother they look for. Someone they think they can control. If they knew you were on a tight watch, it would be different."

"Where . . . where did you come from, Ty? I was about to be done."

"I was going to get some supplies when I saw the crowd outside the school. I looked for you and some girls told me you jetted to the North Side. Something just told me to go looking for you."

Sliding his gaze from the rear view mirror to the exterior side mirrors, Christopher could see that Ty was driving in circles just to keep him company. Spontaneously he ran a few errands in the next town over, made some phone calls and talked about some experiences in his past. When they finally pulled up to Magic Auto Center, it was crowded and cars were steadily moving in.

"You gonna be alright?" Ty asked, palming Christopher's head.

"Yeah. I'ma go work this off."

Ty extended himself toward Christopher and hugged him.

"Stay away from that, understand me?"

"I will. Thanks again, Ty. Later."

"Alright, man."

CHRISTOPER hadn't listened to the news the night before and remembered that Tuesdays were dedicated to current event discussions in history class. He stopped at the newsstand on the corner of Joshua's school and bought the daily paper. The headline read: PRESIDENT: DEMOCRATS PROPOSAL FOR ECONOMIC RECOVERY.

"What's in the news today?" Joshua asked. At his innocent age, the little boy still found joy in going to school. He had not yet struggled with the trials of adolescence or the burden of living without a male mentor—the father Christopher missed every day. He recalled the special moments with his father, particularly when he walked him to school in the mornings.

"You heard me?"

"I don't know yet, I have to read it," Christopher answered, his voice reflecting his distant mind.

"You'll tell me later?" Joshua asked, staring up into his brother's preoccupied eyes.

Pulling on the lid of Joshua's cap, he said, "I'll tell you later, li'l man."

"That's my science teacher," Joshua said, pointing to a young African American woman.

Joshua's school, P.S. 511, was over seventy years old and not fit for the challenges of the new millennium. Christopher spent six years within its confines, and he had very few fond memories of those times. Most notable was the absence of role models that reflected the student population. The school was still resisting change, yet the new make-up of the faculty—a sprinkling of teachers who were people of color—indicated its attempts to try. Inside, students were lined up for breakfast.

"You want anything?"

"Some juice."

"Okay, get on line. Be smart today, li'l man."

"See you later," Joshua said, bumping fists with his brother and then embracing him.

"Love you."

"Love you, too."

Exiting the school building, Christopher's heart dropped into his stomach when he saw that same blue Jeep. He wondered if it were mere coincidence; someone else with a similar vehicle, perhaps. Maybe an Eastern Thug had a younger sibling attending the elementary school. Or maybe he was being followed.

Showing no reaction, Christopher began jogging. When he reached the corner, clear of the Jeep, he ran two blocks up and two blocks over at top speed. He took a shortcut and came upon Telham Park High School from the track field, where team members were performing their morning workouts. Some of them pointed in amazement, following his stride until he stopped. The side entrance that was usually open was locked so he walked around to the front. Never before had he so greatly appreciated the safe haven of Telham Park High School.

AT LUNCHTIME, Christopher joined Deshon and his friends, their plates piled high with meatball parmesan heroes and French fries.

"Whassup?" greeted Deshon.

"Ain't nothin'."

"So what's your plan?"

"Plan for what?" Christopher asked.

"The Eastern Thugs are trailing you," said Alonzo, biting hungrily into his sandwich.

"Y'all writin' a book on this or somethin'?" questioned Christopher.

"We heard they want you," Maverick mumbled, his mouth full of food.

"Huh . . . I want a lot of things."

Deshon shrugged noncommittally and said, "And they'll get you, too."

"I'm not tryin' to get involved in that."

"So when they snatch you up, whatchu gonna do?" asked Alonzo.

Christopher took a healthy bite of his pastrami hero and nodded in approval. "I ain't no punk," he said firmly. "I'ma do what's necessary."

"I know that, but the baddest man can't take on ten."

"But five of us with the Dark Shadows can," grumbled Deshon, almost under his breath.

Christopher looked at Deshon like he had three heads. "What's wrong wit'chu?"

"What's wrong wit'chu?" he replied.

"We hook up with 'em, we untouchable," interjected Maverick.

"That's whassup," agreed Alonzo.

"Yeah, but y'all keep forgettin', you don't just hook up temporarily," Christopher told them. "You gotta be down wit' it all the time. When they fightin' and rumblin', you gotta be down wit' it. You gotta watch their back like they watch yours. So when they start shootin' and killin', you got to get blood on your hands, too."

While digesting the logic of Christopher's words, the noise in the lunchroom seemed to rise.

"Let's git with Jerome," Deshon urged, addressing them all. "What time he got lunch?"

"Sixth," replied Alonzo.

When lunch ended Deshon turned to Christopher. "Meet us in the third-floor bathroom middle of six."

"SIGN IN, take care of your business, exit promptly," instructed the dark, gray-haired security officer who wore a prosthesis in place of his left arm. "Hook"—they called him—guarded the boys' restroom during the afternoon.

It smelled foul inside when Christopher entered. At the third stall door, Christopher recognized Jerome by the back of his towering head and his freestyle Afro. Deshon, Maverick, and Alonzo were positioned at the urinals, pretending to use them. "Yo, yo, I'm in," he announced.

Jerome came out of the stall lighting his clipped cigarette and walked to the open window. As he exhaled, the cold wind pushed the smoke further inside. "So they talkin' about gettin' you, too."

"Yeah," Christopher shrugged. "Said I was one of your brother's boys."

Jerome inhaled a heaping breath of smoke, licked his lips, swallowed, and released the smoke like a pro. Then he took out the pack and handed one to Christopher. "You down with us?"

"Nah . . . I'm not rolling like that. You fightin' 'em?"

"Not alone, I'm not. They want my brother Rob, bad, but he's rolling with the Dark Shadows. Can't get to 'im. That's why they tried to catch him that day with Tevon. But Deshon surprised them. Now they're tryin' to catch me. So we need to be traveling four or five deep."

"You sayin' I gotta be down with the Dark Shadows for protection?"

Jerome made a circle out of the smoke coming out his mouth. "Either that or the Eastern Thugs are gonna hurt you."

All of his friends agreed.

"They already tried once," said Deshon. "Whatchu think they gonna—"

The bathroom door suddenly opened and everybody scattered like mice. Christopher ditched the cigarette in the urinal. Two Puerto Rican juniors, Angel and Richy, came in, speaking in Spanish.

"Psssst," Jerome hissed, bringing them all back together. "Ain't no puzzle, yo. Look, I got somethin' that speaks a universal language. Don't have a name, don't discriminate, and all you gotta do is aim."

Christopher didn't flinch. He knew Jerome had access to guns.

"I can get one for everybody, 'cause my brother got his people over there in—"

Hook did a sneak peek into the bathroom and saw the thick cloud of smoke. "Alright, everybody out," he ordered. "Out!"

Christopher headed to his math class, walking in a daze. Join the Dark Shadows and buy some protection, or become an Eastern Thug. Any way he looked at it he was facing some ugly, undesirable choices.

Avoiding Coach Lappatina was a part of Christopher's daily routine. Ironically, while immersed in his thoughts, he walked right into him on the west corridor of the second floor.

"Young man, I need to talk to you," he said. The ex-Marine and former police officer had the body of an athlete. He was over six feet tall, big and muscular, and well into his forties.

"Coach."

"I saw you running to school this morning. What's goin' on?"

"Nothin'."

"You tellin' me nothing," Coach said, beaming his stern blue eyes on him. "So what's the hurry that time of the morning? I gotta put out an APB, somebody chasin' you?"

"I was running late," Christopher replied, trying to move around him.

"Come back here," said Coach Lappatina and grabbed him by the arm. "See, the problem with you is . . . you run stiff-legged."

"What?"

"Yeah, it's like when you watch a horse run, notice how gracefully he moves."

"You're comparing me to a horse now?"

"Well, you sure as heck can run as fast as one," Coach chuckled, squeezing his neck. "You know what some men would do to have that kind of speed?"

"Not really," Christopher gagged, pretending to be choking.

"But you can't pump your arms and legs like you do."

"Works alright for me."

"Yeah, but you could be better. C'mon, stop playing games with me." The coach turned on his game face. "When are you gonna grow up, huh? You want to be a regular Joe Shmo when you get out there? It's right around the corner, ya know. Gonna live in this neighborhood for the rest of your life?"

"What's wrong with living here?"

"Nothing. But is that what you want for your mother and brother?"

Christopher shrugged awkwardly.

"Do you realize how fortunate . . . the talent you have? You've got a ticket, kid . . . given to you for free." Exaggerating his seriousness, the coach creased his face to a frown. "Why go down the hard way?"

Christopher turned away. The coach then pinned him up against the wall, forcing him to look at him.

"You're fast now, but you could be better. Listen to me. I bet you don't even know how fast you are. Okay, maybe not as fast as Derrick."

"Derrick!" Christopher objected. "I can *crawl* faster than he runs."

"Prove it! C'mon, prove it to me!"

They both laughed at the absurdity of anybody coming close to surpassing his speed. Derrick was known to have the best record on the track team, and he was good—but no match for Christopher.

"Look at me," the coach said, in a low voice. "This is between us. I'll pay you a hundred dollars, out of my own pocket, if you come out to the track tomorrow. I want to see you sprinting so I can test your speed."

"Nah, Coach, you don't have to do that." Christopher was flattered.

"I know, but I want to. I'm serious." His eyes softened and his expression grew sincere. "We just finished up the cross-country races and the team is practicing for the classics now. I want to see you tomorrow . . . or the next day—morning or afternoon—whichever. Hundred dollars is yours. Just be there . . . please."

Christopher looked into Coach's pleading eyes, shook his hand, and headed for class with the thought of escaping the Thugs still weighing heavily on his mind.

three

Christopher arrived at Magic Auto Center early on Friday. After changing into his uniform, he walked outside onto the front lot where the used cars were on display. At every opportunity he checked out the old Mustang turbo convertible that Victor, his boss, had bought at auction several weeks before.

The car was jacked up in the front and the hood was open. With the exception of the body damage to the left rear, it was in great condition. It had low mileage and a good engine, too. Looking at the fiery-red machine, Christopher could see himself and Princess cruising happily around the city and even out of the state. Looking more closely, Christopher bent his body forward to check the condition of the water hose.

"Find some money in there?" asked Victor, approaching him.

"Not yet, boss, but if there's some in here, I'll find it."

With a pad and a pen, Victor took notes, looking along the left side of the car. He was tall and dark, a clean-cut man with Herculean strength. With nineteen-inch biceps, he could make his pectoral muscles dance when he flexed them. A man of few words, Victor was strictly business and he rarely smiled.

"Ay, this engine is clean," Christopher said.

"While you analyzing the hood, get underneath the car and check the condition of the frame. And tell me if there are any leaks in the transmission."

"Underneath?"

"Am I speaking too fast? Get under the car," he repeated, pushing the creeper with his foot toward Christopher. "Sit down and lie flat on your back, just like you do in your bed, and roll yourself underneath."

Christopher positioned himself on the creeper as Victor instructed and rolled slowly underneath the car. It was his first time. He was fascinated by the Mustang's undercarriage.

Victor answered an incoming call on his cell phone and got distracted. "I'm looking at it now," Christopher heard him say. "You can take it as is or we can do some work on it. It's up to you."

"Nothing's leaking from here," Christopher reported after Victor finished his conversation. "I see a little rust. That's about it."

"That's right," Paco, the short, Mexican ace mechanic confirmed. "We just blast, sand and paint . . . and it's good."

"That'll work," Victor said, gripping his pad, "'Cause I got a buyer."

"You gonna sell it?" Christopher asked.

"That's what I bought it for."

"But I thought we were gonna do some work on it first."

"We?" Victor chuckled. "We who?"

"Um . . . everybody here."

"This is a small job. Paco and Roger can knock this out in a day or two," Victor said, moving on to another car.

Christopher wanted the Mustang and he wanted to say so right then and there. But his words got stuck in his throat. He continued working and decided to speak with his boss later in private.

VICTOR'S office was as clean and organized as he was. He was reading with the back of his chair facing the door as Christopher entered. "Excuse me, you got a minute, Victor?"

"Always for you, young fella," he replied, turning around swiftly.

"I wanted to ask you something. Um . . . I was thinking about that car. How much you want for it?"

"Which one?"

"The red Mustang."

"You know somebody who wants to buy it?"

"Yeah."

"Who?"

"Me."

Victor looked crossly at Christopher. "You?"

"Yeah, I want to buy it for my eighteenth birthday."

"You do, huh? What are you going to be doing at eighteen that requires a car?"

"I'll be going to school, working . . . and moving around."

"Think you're ready for that kind of responsibility?"

"Yeah."

"You got the money to buy it and fix it up?"

"Depends on what you're asking for it."

"What about the insurance?"

"That's what I wanted to talk to you about. I was wondering, you know, man to man, maybe we can work something out on that."

"Oh, really," Victor said, swiveling in his chair from side to side. A partial smile came through as he aligned the tips of his fingers and formed a pyramid with his hands. He was amused at Christopher's candor.

"Hear me out, alright. I was thinking I could work for the next eighteen months at half my salary and that would pay for the car. Then, little by little, I could fix it up."

"Okay, but even at working at half your salary that only covers maybe what I paid for the car. Where's my profit?"

Christopher had to think for a moment. "What about extra hours on Saturday with no pay?"

"Okay, but let's look at the time you're talking here. How many months will it be before you're eighteen?"

"Nineteen and a half."

"It's gonna take you all that time to pay me. Now do the math on this. I'm asking thirty-five hundred for the car today. Somebody buys it now and I can turn that money over and buy one or two more cars, double or tripling my money. In a year I could have made ten times that money. If we do it your way, how much money is that?"

"Okay, I make eight dollars an hour," Christopher mumbled, "times three a day. Okay, that's about one-twenty a week. Half of that . . . that's about sixty a week . . . that comes to about two-forty a month."

"With that two-forty a month you giving me, how long would it take to buy a two thousand dollar vehicle—that's how much I paid for it—and that's without repairs and my profit?"

"Not long, um . . . about eight, almost nine months." Christopher slowed down, thinking. "Oh yeah, that is a long time."

"So that's two thousand in eight months as opposed to me making twenty or twenty-five thousand over a year's time. Then what about storage? That car's taking up valuable space every day it sits here. Now the other question is, where you gonna keep it once you buy it and while you're fixing it? I already sat on it for eight months, can't sit on it for another eight."

Christopher contemplated the timeline, unable to come up with any logical answer.

"It's called the 'Time is Money' principle," Victor said. "It's what business is about, Christopher. Learn early."

Recognizing that Christopher looked like a young man whose dreams had just been shattered, Victor offered another suggestion. "Here's a better scenario," he said. "Save your money now in a bank. Draw a little interest from it. Work hard, help me out, and I'll look out for you. Cars are a dime a dozen, man. In nineteen months you won't even be interested in that one. You'll want something totally different." He paused briefly and then continued. "I'll tell you what. When you turn eighteen I'll take you to the dealer's auction with me and you can buy what you want. And when you go to college I'll give you a special deal on any of the parts and labor. Notice I said, *when* you go to college, not *if* you go."

"I heard you."

"Then you'll only have to be concerned with your insurance."

It was a bittersweet suggestion. Christopher wanted that car, but the idea of being able to purchase the vehicle of his choice at an auction thrilled him. He extended his hand excitedly for a shake. Victor's hand was strong and cottony soft. "Okay, you got a deal."

Back in the garage Christopher continued wet-sanding a car when he looked up and spotted the blue Jeep parked across the street. *No, they can't be here. Not where I work.* He hoped real hard that they wouldn't try anything. But if they did, the surprise would be on them because Victor didn't tolerate any nonsense in his place of business.

One time, a group of young guys tried to challenge Victor about a car they'd purchased from him. It was an "As Is" deal. The transmission went out on them after they drove it to Florida and back. The one with the big mouth told Victor he should fix it free of charge. When Victor refused, the guy left and came back to the shop with all his friends. Victor didn't call the cops when he realized trouble was about to erupt. He went into his office and came out holding a bat in his hand. Without a word he leapt toward one of them and swung with such force, catching him on the back, it made the guy holler out like a girl. They all fled after that and never returned.

Maybe the guys in the Jeep are coming to Magic Auto Center as customers. Yeah, that's it. He began sanding in even strokes, keeping his eyes away from their direction. Minutes later, when Christopher looked up, the Jeep had disappeared. He was sure then. The Eastern Thugs knew where he worked and they were watching him.

STAFF DEVELOPMENT training came twice a semester at Telham Park High School, and students attended school only half a day. Christopher and his friends decided against the movies and *the* party—rumored to be a surprise strip teaser requiring a pack of weed or a bottle as admissions—and agreed to meet and go to McCuller's for lunch. When Christopher didn't see them outside, he decided to walk alone to the restaurant, which was only two blocks away.

The small eatery, which sat between the Fairview supermarket and Monticelli's cleaners, had been established in 1959. It was one of the oldest businesses in Telham Park and the only one located two steps beneath the street level. Reminiscent of an earlier time, there were back-to-back booths covered in burgundy plastic, black-and-white photos on the wall, and a jukebox always playing an R&B favorite. Christopher recognized almost everyone in McCuller's, but there was still no sign of his friends.

Angel Rodriquez, a former classmate, sat alone at a table toward the back, fully engaged in his work.

"Hermano!" greeted Christopher, interrupting him. "Que pasa, papa?"

Angel's face burst into a smile. "Whassup, dude? Whatchu doin' here?"

"S'pose to be eatin' with Deshon and my boyz. You seen 'em?"

"Not since I got here."

As Christopher sat down, he waved over at Nadira Watford, Princess' best friend, who sat with three other girls.

"How do you concentrate with all this noise, man?"

"I just tune it out. Besides, I don't know these words anyway."

"What's that, the SAT?"

"It's the practice test, and this thing is kickin', yo."

"But it's a good thing. You score high on it; you got a choice to go to any college you want."

"And what if you don't?"

"See, that's the catch, you gotta score. That's the game they play to keep us separate and apart from the 'haves.' "

"You lost me," Angel said, pushing his glasses up toward his face with his index finger.

"If you want to get into a good college you gotta come up with a score that's off the chain."

"But how many of us do?"

"Not a whole lot. See, the SAT was first put together so everybody could have the same opportunity to go to college. Before that, only the rich white people went to the Ivy League schools 'cause only their kind of high schools were preparing them. But after World War I they invented the intelligence test, calling it 'scholastic aptitude.' Then they developed a school curriculum that was supposed to be fair and prepare everybody for this test."

"Yeah, but our schools don't prepare us for this," Angel rebutted.

"That's the point. They try to tell us that this test measures your natural intelligence, but we know better than that."

"Being intelligent doesn't mean I'm gonna know this stuff. If I'm not taught it and don't practice it, then I'm just gonna look stupid . . . and I'm not stupid," Angel huffed, defending himself. "I got a 94 average, but look at these words. *'Cacophonous: sound, as pungent: odor, tactile: touch.'* How I am supposed to know that? I've never seen some of these words before. And look at this, the reasoning test, check this out: *Melissa Jane Pleasant, as a blank supporter of Black emancipation before the Civil War, spurned politicians who advocated quiet dissent.* Okay, as a what type of supporter? What goes in the blank? That's the question. Is she cavalier, vociferous, sanguine, premature, or noncommittal?"

After a brief pause Christopher said, "I would say she's vociferous."

"I chose sanguine," Angel said, flipping the pages to look up the answer. "You guessed that?" he asked Christopher, puzzled. "Or did you really know it?"

"I just reasoned with it. 'Spurned' I know means like to reject something. 'Quiet dissent' means quiet disagreement, so she would have to be something opposite of quiet disagreement. The only word left that fits is 'vociferous.' "

Exhaling in frustration, Angel continued, "Yeah, but I mean this is not my everyday language. I never use these words. Who would I be talkin' to?"

"That's why a lot of people say it's biased. Look who's making up the test. People from the hood don't use this kind of language, and we're not taught it either. Educated people created it . . . probably scholars. Plus, I think personally, it keeps us scoring lower than anybody else. There's a whole, long history of us underachieving, and tests like the SATs keep the numbers consistent. But don't let that stop you, man."

"I can't," Angel said, shaking Christopher's hand in agreement. "I can't."

"I was reading this book, yo, on natural genius—"

"Whassup," Maverick said, breaking in suddenly. "We were looking for you." Alonzo was with him.

"I was looking for ya'll. Where's Dee?"

"They with the cops in the Dean's office, him and Jerome. I told Rodney to tell you 'cause that's where we were."

"I never saw Rodney," Christopher said, rising up out of his chair. He gave a departing handshake to Angel and he and his friends settled in a booth on the opposite side.

"Y'all eatin'?" Alonzo asked, looking around for a waitress.

"One of the Eastern Thugs got into the building. You heard?" asked Maverick.

"In the school?" Christopher questioned. "For what?"

"That's what the cops wanted to know, and the first person they called was Deshon and then Jerome," reported Alonzo.

"Who was it?"

"They never caught him but when security described him, Jerome confirmed who he was."

"But how did the cops know he was an Eastern Thug?" Christopher probed.

"I don't know," guessed Maverick. "Somebody must have told them."

"But in the school? That's crazy," remarked Christopher.

"Not really, yo, think about it," said Alonzo jumping in. "Once he got inside, he could blend in with the rest of us, find the one he's lookin' for, and smoke 'im right there . . . Then he could run out the back and nobody would ever make the connection. Be somewhere else in no time with a solid alibi."

"Yo, das right," Maverick agreed, bringing his fist down hard on the table.

Alonzo's logical summation alarmed Christopher.

"What are y'all havin'?" asked the waitress, interrupting them.

Christopher spoke first. "Um . . . give me a papaya shake and an order of cheese fries."

"And give me two big joints with cheese, some fries, and a vanilla shake," Alonzo ordered, without ever looking at the short, stout woman.

"Give me the same," said Maverick.

"That's how they move, like rattlesnakes, yo," Alonzo continued. "They can't get Jerome's brother Rob, though. He's rolling with the Shadows all the time, but they can get to his brother in school."

"Yeah, but if they hit Jerome, you talking about war," Maverick declared.

"Psssst, psssst." The sharp, sibilant sound caught Christopher's attention. Nadira was waving excitedly, inviting him to come over to her table. The opportunity to speak about more pleasant topics was a welcome one, so he got up and joined Nadira's group.

All the panic, uncertainty and fear rushed out of him as he sat among his pretty female classmates whose interests were a lot more lighthearted than his.

"You're coming to the Masquerade party Friday, right?" asked Nadira.

"My girl's gonna be there, right?"

"Yes, yes, yes, Christopher, Princess is gonna be there, but I'm telling you now, we're gonna be hanging together. Her aunt's gonna drop her off at her grandmother's and we're leaving from there."

"She's only gonna be home two days, give me some room. You can't monopolize *all* her time."

"What kinda costume you gonna wear?" asked Shakira, a Castilian-brown girl with big, beautiful eyes. She was voluptuous and so top-heavy her breasts rested on the table.

"It's a secret," Christopher said, remembering that he hadn't given his costume any thought.

"Okay, right now I'm trying to organize the final count for Mr. McCuller."

"I thought it was gonna be first-come, first-serve." Christopher asked.

"Not exactly," replied Nadira. "At first they were trying to do like invitation only, but we didn't get a lot of responses. You know how people are. They want to wait to the last minute to do everything. So we're gonna sell as many tickets as we can before the party. The rest of the people will have to pay at the door on a first-come, first-serve basis until we fill up. So you gotta give me twelve dollars now or fifteen at the door."

"Twelve dollars? Whatchu tryin' to do, break a man?"

"You're getting all you can eat and a live DJ too," Lissette mumbled, never raising her head as she punched the calculator keys. She was a good looking girl with Indian features from Panama who spoke fluent Spanish.

"That means I gotta give you twenty-four. I'm paying for Princess."

"Somebody already paid for her," Shakira informed him.

"A look of resentment drew up on Christopher's face. "Who's paying for Princess?" "Psych!" Shakira teased. A burst of laughter sounded out.

Embarrassed, a laugh slowly slipped out of him. "Now why y'all gonna play me like that?"

"Christopher was about to wild out," Lissette said. "So what were you gonna do if it were true?"

"I was gonna find out who it is. That's what I was gonna do."

"What about your friends? Deshon and all of them coming?" asked Nadira.

"Yeah, they'll be there."

"Well, pass the word on, twelve dollars now or fifteen at the door. Deadline's Wednesday."

Just as Christopher stood up, Jerome and Deshon came through the door and walked over to him. Together, they joined Maverick and Alonzo. "What happened?" Christopher asked.

"Ain't nothin'." Deshon answered. "The Dean and the cops call themselves tryin' to intercept a gang fight 'cause of somethin' they heard . . . like what they gonna do about it. By the time they roll up there, it'll be all over."

"Kept us there all that long time askin' us the same questions," Jerome complained, looking over at Deshon. "Yeah, you saw that little cop with the monster ears? Look like a cartoon character, yo. He was tryin' to get me to give up some information on my brother. I was running rings around him and after a while, I was askin' the questions."

"But I'm tellin' you we need to stick tight 'cause I don't know where they comin' from," Maverick warned. He then turned to Deshon and said, "I know you need to chill with that Vanessa 'cause you know how she bend with the wind."

"It's not like she's my girl or nuttin'. I been pumpin' nat for a long time."

"Maybe Big Mo is, too," Maverick said. " 'Cause my sister was at Lashawna's last night and Vanessa lives down the hall. She told me she was standing out in the hallway with those pajama pants on, kickin' it with Big Mo."

"So, what that mean?" asked Deshon.

"It don't mean nothin', but if she swinging from both trees there's gonna be some problems. He might just be pushing up on her to get to you. I don't trust 'im."

"Or, she might be playin' you with a Thug to try to set you up," Alonzo chimed in. "He's older, got that ride and everybody knows he's runnin' things."

Deshon turned away, showing no interest in their speculations.

"He got Bedville all controlled," Jerome said. "They runnin' Ecstasy all up and down there. And they got the baby boys around 511 mulin' it."

"They got the little nine-and ten-year-old kids hustlin'?" Christopher asked. "That's my brother's age." The music stopped playing and they lowered their voices.

"Yo, that's on him what he tryin' to do, but I'm not changing my schedule 'cause of Big Mo," said Deshon, averting his gaze from a girl he watching. "I already know my way around Vanessa. The only thing I gotta do is be ready when the Thugs come for me."

"And I got the perfect companion to accompany you," said Jerome.

The waitress returned to the table and took their orders. After Deshon made his selection, he took some change out of his pocket and passed it to Maverick. "Play my jam *Doggin' the Streets*."

"I was sayin', yo, I got everything we need," Jerome continued, lowering his voice to a husky whisper. "It's at my house. We can go look at 'em now if you want. I'm tellin' you, if you ain't rollin' like that, you naked."

"And what if you get caught with it?" Christopher asked.

"I ain't gonna get caught," Jerome insisted, frowning awkwardly.

"Even if you did," added Alonzo, "better to get caught with protection than to be dead."

A vivid montage of ugly, violent scenes appeared in Christopher's mind. "Why we tryin' to live like gangstas? This is crazy, yo!"

Deshon made several gestures with his hands before any words came out. "It's about protecting this. I already got the wake-up call," he said, pointing to his shoulder.

"The thing is," Jerome explained, "you gotta put fear in them so they stay away from you."

"Yeah, 'cause they're trying to build up the family," said Alonzo. "They even got the little ones poppin' people off with that initiation thing. Ay, remember that lady coming out of her building that time . . . when the little dude just up and shot her? Didn't even wait to see her body drop. He was only twelve."

"I remember that. At least she didn't die," said Christopher.

"Yo," chuckled Jerome. "That's not gonna be my eulogy. I got some stuff for 'em. Y'all coming or what?"

Everybody shook their heads in agreement. They ate their food and headed for Jerome's house.

ONCE OUTSIDE, they lit up cigarettes like men with bad habits. Maverick was the only one who didn't smoke. They stopped on the other side of the boulevard where Dawson's Homes, an urban developer, was building a row of two-family houses.

"Hold up, I want y'all to see this," said Deshon, leading his friends to one of the houses in progress. The foundation had been laid and the shell was attached.

"How long does it take to build one of them?" asked Maverick.

"From start to finish, I give it four to six months," Deshon replied, pressing his face against the glass to see the quality of the workmanship inside.

They compared two of the finished units to the one in progress, admiring the different color schemes and model options. Deshon was absorbed in the particular details of one house when he saw the reflection of two young women pass by.

"Okay, now see, there's some other fine structures right there," he said, eyeballing them. "Foundation is firm. Frame is right. You got different options: sensuous and boob-a-licious, sexy and trim or voluptuous and—"

"You stupid," Alonzo interjected.

Maverick chuckled as he watched them walking. "Them girls was kinda fine, yo."

"See, I'm not the only man that got good eyes." A car swept past them playing music that prompted Deshon into action. He snapped his finger to the fleeting beat and jumped into his creative flow.

"Can a generation nex-a
Be a playa and hex ya
Be ya lover and sex ya
Got the means to protect ya
In the streets represent ya . . ."

The boys arrived at the single-family house on Kenmore Street huffing and puffing from their escape out of the sudden rain shower. They peeled off their wet outerwear, took off their shoes and crowded into

Jerome's disorganized bedroom. Christopher cleared a place on the bed, turned on the television, and switched to The History Channel.

Jerome dug between stacks of shoeboxes and pulled out a white-and-blue sneaker box. Inside laid three guns. "This one will take you out," he said, picking up the first weapon. It was a hard-chrome-plated.25 semi-automatic pistol.

Each one of them held the steel as they made mental notes. "This could fit right in my pocket," said Maverick.

When Alonzo held the gun, he aimed it at Christopher. "Ay yo, this is what you call instant gratification."

Christopher turned around and did a double take, staring into the barrel of the weapon. "Get that outta my face, yo!" They all laughed.

"Bullets in here?" Alonzo asked Jerome.

"No. It's got the safety lock on anyway."

He passed it to Maverick, who examined the length of the barrel. "Now dis here is what I'm talkin' 'bout."

"But those are small," Jerome said, comparing the three of them. "That one's the .25, this one's a .22, and this one's a .40. Look what else he got." He pulled a tennis racket case out of the closet and unzipped it. Carefully wrapped inside of a white towel was a 9mm. "This is my brother's."

Amazed, their eyes grew large and silence inched between them as they examined the weapon carefully. The only sound was The History Channel television announcer's voice, describing the details of the effects of beta and gamma radiation exposure in the Hiroshima bomb explosion.

"How much they want for it?" Alonzo asked Jerome.

"Like four, five hundred for these. But some of 'em go higher than a grand."

Maverick was curious about the cartridge capacity of the .22 semi-automatic and asked, "How many rounds does this magazine hold?"

"Enough to stop you *dead* in your tracks," Deshon replied. Fascinated by the lethal power of the firearm he held, a sinister smile grew on his face. "Yeah, I can work with this."

"And do what with it?" Christopher asked.

"Make it do what it needs to do," he answered and smacked hands with Jerome.

Christopher was drawn back to the television program, listening attentively while occasionally watching his friends. Interested in the .25 automatic, Alonzo measured its ability to be concealed. He placed it inside his pants on the right side and then on his left and walked around the room trying to get a feel for it. Maverick held the .22 and simply profiled it as if it were a new shirt or sweater. Jerome cleaned the gun and practiced dismantling it, a seemingly pointless exercise.

Christopher sat amid an environment of violence: The History Channel's television program was exposing the gory details of chemical warfare. In the same room his friends were conspiring to use deadly weapons in personal warfare. He looked forward to moving on to more civilized surroundings.

four

C hristopher felt sluggish walking on the asphalt of Telham Park's High School's track so early in the morning. At six thirty-two a.m., beneath the overcast sky, the air was chilly in the quiet city. He sipped on his second cup of caffeinated green tea to wake up from the foggy reality; a disdain of violence and gangs and an everyday existence he cared to be no part of, still whirling in his head.

Remembering his father's companionship, he could almost hear his footsteps walking beside him. "I miss you so much, Dad," he murmured. "Feels strange out here without you. Remember how we used to run in the park? Maybe that's why I can't get excited about the sport. 'Cause you're not here with me." Christopher looked up to the gray sky and thought he heard a reply, *"But I am always with you."*

Coach Lappatina looked startled when he saw Christopher coming toward him. Then, with a smile so wide it revealed all his front teeth, he threw his arms around him lovingly, like a father would. "What is this? We're on a half-day schedule," he said. "You should have been here two hours ago."

"Two hours ago?" Christopher frowned, perplexed. "The sun wasn't even up yet."

"Yeah, and look," he pointed to the sky. "It's still not up, so what does that have to do with you starting your day? You can run in the dark just like you do when it's light, son. That's what winners are made of. Haven't you figured that out yet?"

"Nah."

"Ay, less distraction before daybreak," he countered, dragging his eyes over the field.

"But Coach, why do I—"

"Okay, look, you're here; this is good. Drop the bag, take off your coat, and let's get started."

Members of the track team were running their daily laps around the track. The football players were doing jumping jacks and stretches in the middle of the field, led by Coach Stuben.

Coach Lappatina was so fired up he could hardly stand still. He didn't seem as tough or as serious as he was during school hours.

"Okay, Chris, you ready?"

"Um hum."

"Hey, what are these?" he asked, pulling at the material of Christopher's pants. He was wearing his velour two-piece warm-up suit.

"What's wrong with these?"

"Well, they're not exactly the kind of pants made for sweating. Oh . . . oh, I get it. You want to run and look good at the same time. Okay, I'll let it go this time. Now get out there and give me two laps!"

Christopher jerked his head back. "Two laps?"

"You gotta get loosened up."

"I'm already loose."

"C'mon, c'mon, be a good son," schmoozed the coach. "Give me two laps and after that, I'm gonna time you on the hundred."

Running on the wide-open track was a liberating experience for Christopher. Moving at moderate speed, he found himself wrapped in thoughts of the future. Where would he be two years from now? Five years? What kind of money would he be making designing cars? At what age would he and Princess get married? He indulged his thoughts in all the things he wanted in life and imagined having them.

One complete lap around the track equaled a quarter of a mile. He could feel the strain in his legs, and his upper body began to feel heavier. *This running thing is not as easy as it looks.* Keeping up the pace now required more effort. That's when he felt the vulnerability of competing out in the open. He had no desire to have people gawking at him while exerting painstaking energy striving to get to a finish line. He ran past the football team, whose members were running in place. He swept past the school building and then continued on around the track, where he could see the street.

"You warmed up now?" Coach Lappatina asked when he returned.

"Yeah," Christopher answered, breathing heavily. His insides felt like they were on fire.

"Okay, I want you to do a hundred-meter sprint. Got that?"

"Just tell me when."

"Set your watch," said Coach Lappatina to Coach Stuben who had joined them. He was a big pale-pink man with light brown hair, a former college All-American football player himself. "I want you to see this."

"Isn't that the kid who—"

"That's my boy. Show us what you workin' with, Christopher. Ready?"

"Yeah," Christopher replied as he settled into the blocks.

"On your mark . . . get set . . . go!"

Propelling his body forward with effortless, measured strides, Christopher ran the hundred meters and crossed the finish line in no time.

Coach Lappatina looked at his watch and locked eyes with Coach Stuben. "*Holy Mother of Christ!* You witnessed it too; I'm not dreaming."

"Impossible," said Coach Stuben, reading the stopwatch.

"This kid is not this fast," Coach Lappatina mumbled, still in disbelief. "Tell me we just struck gold."

"Uh, Chris . . . we need you to try it again," Coach Stuben insisted.

"What's the matter, timing is slow? Been a long time since I did any running."

Neither coach commented. They were busy synchronizing their stopwatches and moving to opposite ends of the finish line.

Christopher got into position again. He looked straight ahead with both hands touching the ground. This time he felt more prepared, a competitive drive creeping upon him.

"On your mark . . ."

Christopher swayed back and forth on the strength of one leg.

"Get set . . ."

His mind was focused, determined to finish in better time.

"Go!"

Christopher took off like a rocket, remembering how his father taught him.

"Good start," Coach Stuben acknowledged.

Now, with warmer muscles and a mission in mind, Christopher's arms propelled his body forward and his feet stamped the asphalt, defying the winds in record time. The football team watched in astonishment as he flew past them.

The coaches clicked their stopwatches the second he stepped across the finish line. Coach Lappatina hurried toward Coach Stuben with a look of disbelief.

"Nine-point-six," both coaches said simultaneously.

"That kid just ran the hundred in 9.6 seconds," Coach Stuben stated incredulously.

"We haven't even worked him yet," Coach Lappatina observed, running his fingers briskly through his hair. "Christ! This guy's a living legend and he doesn't even know it. Let me talk to him."

Christopher was breathing heavily but felt exhilarated after the rigorous sprint.

"You did good, Chris, but your speed . . . could use some improvement."

"What's my time?"

"That's not important right now. I know you can do better," Coach Stueben affirmed, nodding his head.

A feeling of disappointment crept into the pit of Christopher's stomach. He felt he had done really well, and besides, he actually *liked* the feeling of running. How had he forgotten?

"Ya gotta practice, son. Develop your legs. Build up your upper body strength so you can increase your speed. But it takes time . . . four to five years. I mean it's already late in the game, but you have an advantage."

"What's that?"

Coach Lappatina's eyes narrowed at the question. "You're faster than anybody else, that's the advantage. So what are you gonna do, kid? Time is winding up."

Christopher bent his head to the right, looking over the field. "I don't know, Coach, I'm not feelin' it right now . . . and I don't want to make any promises I can't keep."

"You're not feeling it because you're not prepared. C'mon." Coach Lappatina took Christopher by the shoulder and they began to walk. "Talk to me. What do you think your father would have wanted for you?"

Christopher's eyes scanned the field. "I don't know. Guess he would have wanted . . . the best for me."

"You guessed right. Then why aren't you doing your best? I talk to your teachers. They tell me you're givin' them crap in the classroom."

"I'm passin'."

"So is every other average guy. What's up with that?"

Christopher didn't have an answer, not a reasonable one anyway, and allowed his eyes to wander. "Things are rough right now and—"

"You forget? I know what you can do. If you're passing, that means you're not studying because I know what you have up there in that brain. So imagine what you'd being doing with a little effort. No, a lot of effort, we don't do little. Am I right? Would your father tell you do a little?"

" . . . No."

"Look at me," he said and stopped. "I'll tell you what. Pick up your grades; I'll put you on the team."

"I don't know, Coach . . . not right now."

"So tell me when?" Pointing down to Christopher's legs, he asked, "Do you realize those are pure platinum for your future? We're talking trophies and medals, a scholarship to college, even the Olympics. That's money, r-e-c-o-g-n-i-t-i-o-n, my dude. Feel me?"

Christopher gave off a spirited laugh. Coming from the coach, street slang sounded peculiar.

"Funny, huh?" Soon a smile broke and he pulled Christopher closer to him. "Do you know how proud you could make your mother?"

"Maybe, but I'm just not into it, Coach. I go to school, I work, gotta pick up my little brother and then this. I don't want nobody depending on me and then I—"

"Then what?" The coach stopped and pointed his head toward the street. "You got more important business out there? More important than your future?"

Christopher avoided his eyes and set them on the football team doing another round of jumping jacks.

"Ay, I'm a tough guy. Want to break me down? That's what you'll do if something happens to you out there in the streets."

Christopher's gaze returned to Coach Lappatina.

"Look, you've got the foundation, kid, and your heart is in the right place. C'mon, how many kids your age make a promise and keep it? You didn't have to come here this morning, but you did. Maybe that's telling you something."

"Not really, I was just—"

"I know you're going through changes, guy. I've been there. It's tough, but so are you. I think you're a good kid—no, a *great* kid. Ay listen, your teachers think so, too. School, that job, your brother—we can work it all out . . . and you can join the team."

Christopher bent his upper body forward and gripped his knees, thinking. He thought about the rigorous practicing schedule, track meets and the demands of school. His lifestyle would drastically change.

The coach looked away and blew his whistle, signaling team members to assemble. While Christopher gazed at the ground, the coach placed a hundred-dollar bill in front of his face. Christopher rose up, the sun now peering through the dull clouds. "What's this?"

"I'm keeping my word."

"C'mon, Coach. You don't have to do that," Christopher said, his face creased in a frown, as if he had been insulted.

"A deal is a deal. Here." The coach shoved the bill toward Christopher's pocket.

Christopher backed off quickly. "Don't play with me, Coach."

"You kept your word and now I'm keeping mine. Here, take it."

"Nnn...now I'm calling the shots and I say we're even."

The coach tried to put the bill in Christopher's hand and he backed off even further. "You playin' yourself, Coach. I told you it's cool. I'm good."

Neither of them were bending. As the students began to assemble, the coach discreetly folded the bill and put it back in his pocket.

"You joining us?" Christopher heard one of the team members ask.

He looked at the coach and saw disappointment. He stepped away gradually and said, "I'll see you around."

"Yeah, we'll talk."

THE KITCHEN table was cluttered with books and papers at the Murphy home the next evening. Christopher was reading two books at a time about the life of Frederick Douglas. Along with his homework, Joshua had an art project to complete—one using a historical theme.

"What'd you do, li'l man, trace these pictures?" Christopher asked, teasing him.

"Picture that," replied Joshua. "These are all original."

"It's good to listen to your big brother. I told you this was the way to go."

"Yep, you did. All I have to do now is color them."

Christopher turned on an additional light in the ceiling fan to examine the work more carefully. For the art exhibition at school, Joshua had drawn pictures of objects invented by African Americans. He had an uncanny talent for duplicating any figure he studied with the delicate stroke of his left hand.

"Whoa, you did good with these." Christopher praised, checking over each picture. "You got the doorknob, the light switch, the refrigerated truck, the traffic light, the golf tee, the gas mask, and this is, um . . . J.M. Certain's thing, the bicycle basket." Christopher studied the last picture from several angles. "What's this one li'l man?"

"It's the third rail."

"Third rail? Hmm . . . you need to highlight this one some more. And who invented it?"

"Granville T. Woods. He invented the roller coaster, too."

"That's what I'm talking about!" Christopher raised his right hand to give Joshua a high five and he received it with a crackling smack.

"What about Carver and Benjamin Banneker?"

"Oh shoot, where did I—" Joshua went into his room and returned with several more drawings. "Here's Benjamin Banneker's clock and Carver's bleach."

"Banneker invented more than just the clock."

"I know, I know. He invented shaving cream and coffee."

"No, he didn't invent coffee itself," Christopher clarified. "He invented the way to make it instant."

"I knew that."

"Uh huh, now where are the inventors' names and information? You got to attach it to the pictures."

As Joshua searched through his backpack, the phone rang.

"Hello . . . Speakin', who's calling?" He turned his back to his little brother, mumbling quietly.

Joshua opened his folders and the big gold letters that would entitle his exhibition fell out. He suddenly realized he was missing one of them. Joshua could tell his brother was talking to a girl so he nudged him and whispered, "I left my other folder at Lou Lou's. I need to go get it."

"That girl is on another planet," Christopher said, hanging up the phone. "I don't know what she keep callin' me for."

" 'Cause you gave her your number."

"I did not."

"How'd she get it then?"

"Probably one of my friends."

"You know you gave it to her," he said, giggling. "You know you like her."

"Yeah, okay. Just keep coloring those pictures. I'll go get your stuff."

Before leaving the building Christopher checked in on Pop-Pop. He helped him find some missing screws to an old lamp that he was trying to fix. Then he jogged the few blocks with Coach Lappatina on his mind. He entertained thoughts about becoming a track star, the awards he could win, the glory he could bring to Telham Park High School, and how proud his mother would be. But he also knew that things that didn't interest him didn't hold his attention for long. There they were, the opposing men living inside of him. His father often told him, "One of the greatest battles you'll ever gonna encounter in your life, son, is the battle within yourself."

He started up the stairs at Lou Lou's when he heard a succession of violent screams. Then came a thunderous rumble of footsteps tearing down the stairs. Six or seven young men wearing hoods came running like fire. Christopher moved to the side, and out of the way of the stampede. He then kneeled down and watched them through the stair railings, trying to see who they were. He noted a peculiar birthmark on the face of one of them who peeled off his hood before shooting out the front door.

By the time Christopher had moved up the stairs there was a crowd circled around Santos Martinez, who was pinned against the third floor stairwell. He was a Puerto Rican teenager, about seventeen, who worked in the corner bodega.

"Dios mio! Que pasa?" one woman screamed when she saw him bleeding from the side of his head, nose and mouth.

"Llama la policia!" another one yelled, scrambling to comfort Santos.

"Did anybody see them?" asked an older black man wearing a white T-shirt. He lived in the building; Christopher had seen him before.

Lou Lou came out of her apartment and was startled when she saw Christopher. "What are you doing here?" She was an older, fair-skinned plump woman with a loose tongue.

"Joshua left his folder and I came to get it. Then I saw these guys runnin'—"

"You saw what happened?" she whispered, looking above her half-eyeglasses.

"Los morenos," a young girl cried, stealing everyone's attention.

"What does that mean?" Lou Lou asked.

"Some Black boys did it," a Hispanic man replied.

Santos struggled, in his semi-delirious state, to explain. "Somebody kept knocking. They wouldn't show their face. When I opened the door they grabbed me."

"Dios mio, Dios mio!" his mother screamed, terrified at the sight of her son's face. His father was right behind her, muttering erratically in Spanish. Christopher couldn't understand exactly what he was saying, but whatever it was, it was obscene.

Santos's words were muffled as his mother pressed a cloth up against his mouth to stop the bleeding. "I couldn't see them. They dragged me over here and started beating me . . . and stuck a gun in my mouth." Like a baby he began to weep. "And they took my chain."

Pity for Santos poured out of Christopher for he knew what they had done, and even more frightening, he knew who they were. Stung by what he had seen, Christopher walked home cautiously holding the folder, taking nothing in his surroundings—sound or movement—for granted. He welcomed the cold air rushing into him, soothing his burning head. *What if they saw me? Are they gonna come after me like that?*

Gilroy was playing a delicate, tender solo as Christopher walked up the stairs in his building. He took his time and settled into its soothing melody. Once in his apartment he put the incident out of his mind and said nothing about what happened. Gilroy's distant horn riffs had lulled him into a thoughtful mode. After Joshua finished his project, Christopher wanted to get out, but not back on the street.

"Hey Mom, I'm going downstairs to Gilroy's. I'll be back."

A FAMILIAR kind of tranquility came over Christopher as he entered Gilroy's apartment, smelling of spicy nutmeg and ginger and all the distinct aromas of Jamaican cuisine. "Come in my boy, come, come." Mrs. Harker, his mother greeted him, reaching up to embrace Christopher. She was a short, portly woman with bright eyes and a warm heart. "Gilroy in *him* room."

In their little foyer sat an old Baldwin piano that always caught Christopher's attention. On top of it sat family photos, vintage candleholders, and a Jamaican flag.

The sound of the horn grew louder when Christopher stepped inside the swanky furnished bedroom-turned private studio. Gilroy worked in the corner with just the chair he sat in, his musical stand, and his trumpet.

Christopher made himself comfortable on the black futon sitting underneath the radiance of sleek track lighting, while examining photographs of Miles Davis, Wynton Marsalis, Louis Armstrong, Dizzy Gillespie and some other famous trumpeters.

"*Supercat. Whas de rhydem?*" Gilroy asked suddenly, rising up. He was short and dark with coal-black eyes that looked like they could burn a hole through you.

"Ain't nothing, man, hi you," Christopher replied as they shook hands and embraced.

"Cool, cool."

"I heard you playin' so I thought I'd come down and holla. I'm not disturbing you, am I?"

"No, no, just practicing, jazzin' it up a little," Gilroy replied, smiling, showing his big white teeth.

"You got a show or something coming up?"

"Always a show, but I have to practice for me. I'm working on some new pieces."

"What were you playing earlier?"

Gilroy thought for a moment. "Light blues."

"It sounded like that New Orleans, early 1900s jazz."

"Good ear, boy! Jazz is just another way of playing the blues. I was mimicking the master, Louis Armstrong. You know him?"

"Satchmo?" Christopher replied, settling back on the futon. "'Course I do. That seemed like a good time to be livin' in, right?"

"*De bess*. And New Orleans . . . *de* city of music."

"Yeah, they was partying in the honky tonks and speak-easies back then. Yo, nothing but good music, dancing, and women. Just like today, really. History just repeats itself . . . and picks up new flava along the way."

"You're right. Things evolve constantly. A 'B' flat is always a 'B' flat, but it's the style of the musician carrying it."

"So how do you sit here and practice all the time like you do?" Christopher asked. "I mean, you practice religiously . . . every day . . . for hours."

Gilroy blew a few bars as he was thinking. "I'm reaching for a new level. And by practicing I stretch myself."

"But what makes you love it?"

Gilroy ripped into a snappy, upbeat melody, twisting and bending notes and stopped. "You mean, why the trumpet?"

"Yeah."

"I thought about it," he replied. "But I believe it chose me."

"So what, you just woke up one morning and said you gonna play?"

"No. Nothing comes that easy. I tell you, *bock* in Jamaica we lived modestly, more like poor, so we had to make our own entertainment. *Me* toys was twigs, or pebbles, or rocks. I used to watch my *fadda's* friend play when they did the little sessions on Friday for the tourists. *Me fadda* played the piano, but his friend Sorrow . . . he could make the trumpet talk, sometimes cry, or moan in agony. It amazed me! I used to think it was magic, but when he showed me how to be the magician I felt like I had found a partner, my own special friend." He gazed at the trumpet like it was something good to eat.

"*Me mudda* save all she tips from *de* hotel and bought me a used horn. It was tarnished and old, had some dents in it, but in my eyes . . . I saw gold. Now, we have an understanding. Makes me practice real hard before I can get it right. It *neva* come easy. Sometimes I want to *trow* it away, but it won't let me. Then sometimes I miss it; you crave it like you do a girl, *mon*."

Christopher marveled at the way Gilroy turned his accent on and shut it off in between sentences, and he loved the rhythm of Gilroy's speech, a unique Jamaican/New York mix. "Okay, what if you felt like that about playing, but it wasn't in you or you didn't have the talent or ability?"

"That's why I say it choose me. My *fadda* passed on the music, *in me blood now*, but it don't mean I'm gonna find my way *wid* it. But I give it a chance, worked with it and soon I fall in love. *Hoppened* early and I'm nine years now playin'."

Christopher sat silently digesting Gilroy's words.

"You feel heavy, *mon*," Gilroy said, out of the blue.

"What?"

"Heavy, you feel. *Bock* home some say, 'What *ailin'* ya, boy?' "

Christopher chuckled admiring the photos of Miles Davis. "Sometimes I feel like my father's still here, just on a vacation or somethin'. Then other times I know . . ." He stared off, as if gazing into some faraway existence.

"Your *fadda's* always with you. Like my *granfadda's wid* me. Angels are powerful *ya* know."

"Check this out," Christopher said. "I met with the coach in my school the other day, right? He's always beatin' on me about joining the track team. So I go up there, do a little something for him; I'm talking with no effort at all. The way I see them out there practicing hard every morning, yo . . . I don't have to do none of that, know what I'm sayin'?"

"Yeah *mon*."

"So the coach is trying to tell me that my time could be better, but I know he just psyching me up. C'mon, for me, runnin' is—" Christopher gestured with the snap of his finger. "But I don't feel this passion for it . . . like you do with the trumpet. I don't get worked up over the thought of running. I mean, what am I running for?"

"What do we do anything for?" Gilroy's comeback was immediate. "To get something in return, right? It may not be burnin' in your belly, but use it to stretch you and get to the next level."

"I hear you."

"Anyway, you'll be running for somebody one day—a job, the wife and family—so you might as well do you first. Look, some get one gift, some get five."

Christopher nodded and quoted the familiar passage of the Bible: "But the one given only one gift can do better than the one with five, if it's used right."

Gilroy smiled again. "Sometimes you can do two, maybe *tree tings* well, don't mean you want any of *dem*, but look at *de* blessing in having the choice."

Mrs. Harker entered the room suddenly, carrying two plates of carrot cake. "For you," she said, giving each of them the dessert. She practiced what she preached, believing that boys were always willing to eat, so offering them food was a waste of breath. She simply prepared the portions.

"Mmm, thank you," Christopher said, eyeing it gratefully.

"I got tea, milk, *wata*—"

"No ma'am, this is good, but thank you."

"Gilroy tell you who him gonna play *wid*?" she asked, looking over his desk area and tidying his papers.

"No," Christopher replied, tasting the moist, delicious cake as it melted in his mouth.

"Starting next *munt* him gonna study *wid* Ray Field," she proudly announced and left the room.

"Makin' it do what it do, yo! Congratulations! You mean I'm talkin' to the next Wynton Marsalis?"

"Don't know about that," Gilroy shrugged, "But I'm grateful for the chance to learn from the best."

That's good, man! I'm happy for you."

When Gilroy finished his cake he walked over to his computer and collected some music sheets. One of his legs was longer than the other, so when he walked he swayed on his right side. When walking slowly his handicap was barely noticeable, but when Gilroy walked in a hurry, he moved slightly like a penguin.

"So, you excited?"

Gilroy smiled and picked up his trumpet. He began playing a blues tune with long, stretched notes filled with tension. A new birth arose in the ennobled sound, a human energy shooting out to the universe.

Christopher closed his eyes and listened until Gilroy paused. "You comin' out of the Harlem Renaissance now, early 1920s. I can almost see that time . . . artistic explosion."

"Yeah, *mon*."

"So happy to be free. Can you imagine that sojourn from the dreaded South? Dehumanized and brutalized all their lives and suddenly, loosened from the chains. So you got your freedom, yeah, with nothing else but the clothes on your back. Then you make that journey to the North hoping to find a job and you can't even read."

Gilroy bobbed his head in agreement. He played on and on and then stopped abruptly at his revelation. "Maybe that's what's choosing you."

"What?"

"Your head is a history book, *mon.*"

Christopher looked oddly at Gilroy. "Why do you say that?"

"It's all you talk about. But even *furder dan dat,* you have a perspective on it, an opinion. Like when you was telling me about the invasion of Cuba back in the '90s, when all those people were blown away."

"Nah," Christopher interjected. "That was the invasion of Panama . . . in the late '80s, when the war on drugs was heavy. Bush ordered that invasion. Had the military kill all those innocent people to find Noriega—one man, who was on the payroll of the CIA and—"

"See my point." Gilroy released a satisfied grin. "You're good. In time you will be a Cornell West, but you gotta work hard for this."

"It's funny you say that, but all my friends think I'm bugged. They want me to be down with them."

"That's where they are." Gilroy frowned in disregard.

"And the gangs, yo. Dudes are lookin' for me now." A scowl appeared on Christopher's face, changing the mood.

"Whatchu tellin' me?"

"They want me to be down with 'em."

"Why?"

"I don't know. I don't mess with thugs. Like that situation I saw earlier." Christopher paused, nodding vigorously. "They went to work on Santos, this Spanish dude I know. He real cool, yo. For no reason they beat 'im down, stuck a gun in his mouth and robbed him. I just happened to be in the building and saw them running out. Couple of seconds sooner—"

"You told the cops?"

"I look stupid? I'm not tryin' to get involved with that."

Gilroy fixed his gaze on Christopher as he processed the information. "You got to elevate yourself from *dat*."

"But this is where I live . . . who I am. Why I gotta make a move?"

"Me *granfadda* always told me you got to meet a situation head-on, wrestle *wid* it. One *ting* don't work, you try *anada*."

"What I gotta do is protect myself."

"How so?"

"However I have to," Christopher responded, eyes gleaming in staunch resolve.

"*Whad de ras mon*? Gilroy disapproved, sucking on his teeth so strongly they sizzled. "You fallin' into *de* trap," he said and laid his trumpet down across his lap. "Okay, look at me. I'm a good-looking guy . . . some say."

They chuckled together enjoying the momentary humor.

"*De* girls don't mind *afta* me '*cept* when I'm playin'. One foot *shotta dan de odder*, but *me* world is full *wid dis*," he explained, picking up his trumpet. "When I'm playing I'm *eidder* here, *dare o dare. Dem dare* people wouldn't come near to my circle. You know why?" Gilroy sneered, laid his trumpet back down and balled up his fist. "Because I'll box *dem heads and mash 'em up*."

Now they were laughing.

"Serious. You know why? Because *dey* don't belong *dare*. Dey don't have dreams, not even hope. Look around here. Not *de bess*, but big, big *tings* is comin'. When I come *tru*, *dem* cats move aside. Limpin' and all, they don't *bodder* me. Nah, *mon*, *dem* can't relate because I elevate . . . but nothin' you do separates you from *dem*."

"But I can do what I want to do."

Gilroy picked up his trumpet and played a wailing, sardonic sound. It whirled through the length of the room like it was bobbing and weaving anchorlessly in the midst of an angry sea. Then he stopped. "So can *dey* . . . and you know where *dey* going?" Gilroy pointed his left thumb down toward the floor. "And they *guan* take every soul down *dare* with *dem*. Make people miserable because *dis* is *dare* power. It's wicked, *mon*. *Brudas have too many problems, why* complicate *tings* more? But *dey* never elevate."

This time Gilroy eased into a solo cadenza entrenched in melodic swirls and polyphonies. Christopher listened as he stared transfixed at the blank wall.

"Put one foot in front of the other," Gilroy advised upon an abrupt stop. "Start with ten minutes a day. If you gonna run, give it *everyting*. Then a little more each day. Same with your reading. You won't find *dem* guys in the library or the track field. And ask the ONE above to give you strength. Your *fadda* will help you, too."

Gilroy's words hung in the air as he careened into an instrumental version of Luther Vandross' *So Amazing* that seemed to last for some time. Christopher settled back into his thoughts as if he were the only one in the room. He could see himself and his father fishing so vividly. As the sound of the trumpet played on, Christopher picked up their cake plates and exited as quietly as he had entered.

five

Church had become the party in the Murphy household on Saturday evening with an even mix of traditional and contemporary uplifting gospel playing as the savory aroma of barbeque beef ribs wafted through the air. Eager to get the Masquerade party at McCullers, Christopher got dressed early. He was fond of the gold studded royal blue velvet cape and matching jeweled gold crown. Mrs. Murphy initially made the costume when he played the role of an Egyptian Prince for Black History Month in junior high school and altered it to fit. Completing the look, Christopher put on his sunglasses that all his friends agreed to wear and looked in the mirror. *Yeah, that'll work. Princess will love this.*

"The cape fits you well," Mrs. Murphy said, beaming at his regal appearance.

"Yep, and it's a good look, Mom." In the mirror he could see his mother holding hard to a half-smile and a distant stare. Christopher knew that look. His mother would sometimes escape into a trance, recalling the springtime of her life.

When the phone rang, Christopher went into the kitchen to answer it. "Hello . . . Hello . . . Hello . . ." The handset hit the base hard, a sign of his growing impatience. "That's the third time somebody called here and hung up."

"That's probably that ugly girl that likes you," Joshua teased, admiring his handsome brother.

"How you know?"

"That's what girls do sometimes . . . 'specially if they scared. She probably wanna ask you somethin', but she scared you might say no 'cause she ugly."

"What did I tell you about calling *anybody* ugly?" chided Mrs. Murphy. "Everything God made is beautiful."

"Uh huh," Christopher agreed. "That's what our people used to be called all the time."

"And now we're calling ourselves ugly," Ms. Murphy added. "Not in this house, though. Understand me?"

"Yes," Joshua replied, making silly, comedic gestures at Christopher when his mother turned her head. "I'm just sayin', those are the kind of girls that like to call and hang up."

Christopher wanted to believe that it was a girl, but a pang of anxiety struck him with a warning that it might be someone else. Then he dismissed it.

BY THE TIME Christopher arrived at McCuller's with Deshon, the party was in full gear. Beneath the dim lights the air crackled with excitement, booming music and hordes of girls.

Christopher felt especially proud of his costume among the pirates, gangsters, and cowboys. Deshon was dressed like a pimp out of the '70s with a wide-brimmed hat, a maxi coat with fur around the collar, and bell-bottom pants. He, too, wore dark glasses.

"It's about time," Tamika said, coming up from behind. Made up like a gypsy, she had on a long black wig, big hoop earrings, false eyelashes, and a beauty mark drawn right above her lip.

It was an improvement to her looks, Christopher thought. But the sensuous drawl in her voice and the sleepy batting of her eyes was no put-on. He could tell she'd been drinking.

"Can you guess?" she asked, as she modeled her costume.

"Is that you . . . Tamika?" Christopher gazed, feigning interest.

She grinned from ear to ear, sliding her hand through his arm. "Come sit at the table with us?"

"Nah, nah. I just got here and I'm looking for somebody."

Tamika turned away, disappointed. That's when Christopher spotted Jerome. He towered over the crowd wearing a purple jacket, baggy pants, a sombrero, curled mustache, and sunglasses. Alonzo, standing next to Jerome, was the man dressed in black—the suit, the shirt, the tie, and the glasses. With his serious demeanor and gelled hair pulled back into a ponytail, he resembled a hit man. Deshon pointed Maverick out, who merely looked like himself wearing a hat turned backwards and dark sunglasses. Christopher and Deshon walked to the rhythm of the music across the floor to meet them when they bumped into Vanessa. In a skimpy leopard ensemble, a miniskirt and a midriff blouse, Vanessa had no inhibitions about showing off all her jewels.

"That's where I need to be," said Deshon. "But I'ma look around first."

"You playin' on Vanessa," Christopher asked."

"She know the rules, yo. I'm not wit nobody when—"

"Y'all just got here?" Jerome jumped in suddenly. His full lips were more pronounced with the false mustache dancing up and down as he spoke.

"That cape is you, dawg!" Jerome praised Christopher. "You got enough room in there to carry anything you want, know what I'm sayin'." Jerome and Deshon exchanged glances.

Christopher ignored them, knowing the direction they were going and turned to Alonzo who hands were already wrapped around a lovely Dominican girl named Daniella. His gaze shifted toward the door just in time to see Princess entering the restaurant. Radiant, she wore a long white gown, a winter-white shawl, and a tiara that sparkled with a rainbow of colors.

"Lightning!" Princess hailed, opening her arms to receive him.

"Oooh, look at them," one girl cooed, admiring Christopher and Princess' appearance as royalty. "Did y'all plan this?"

"No, not at all," Princess replied.

"Buttah, Buttah, Buttah," he said, embracing her and then lifting her up in the air. "You haven't changed at all."

Princess laughed merrily as he swung her around. "What did you expect in six or seven weeks?"

Christopher was gloating. "You look real good!"

Princess made haughty little gestures associated with royalty to excited friends who gathered nearby. Christopher couldn't resist adding a smidgen of comedy to the festivities. He bowed to 'Her Majesty' on one knee, and Princess curtsied in response. After a brief kiss to her hand, he stood tall and offered her his elbow. Laughing in appreciation, their friends applauded their improvised routine as they moved to the dance floor.

"Whassup, Buttah?"

"Ah, my Prince Charming, what's going on?"

His white teeth glowed against his brown skin as he searched her lovely face. With her hair pulled away from her face in tight curls, her strong features were prominently displayed. "I missed you," he said with a light peck to her full, glossy lips.

"Don't start on me, Chris."

"But I must. I'll never stop." He tightened his grip around her and did an easy two-step, ballroom style.

"All right now. "Who taught you how to dance like this?" Princess asked.

He looked into her clear, sparking brown eyes and spoke. "C'mon, ain't too many things I don't know how to do." He brought her close and swung her around in their tight space, bent down to her ear, and said, "I got you now . . . and I'm not lettin' go."

"You still the same, Chris."

"Same ole, same ole."

Minutes later an upbeat rhythm jolted their slow dance and they entered into a new groove. Princess touched Christopher's cape and rubbed it between her fingers. "Now what made you choose this?"

"I don't know. At first I was gonna maybe wet myself up in some baby oil, get naked and come out wearing a thong. Nah, I'm just playin'," he laughed. "I was looking for something different. I don't know, maybe it was a sixth sense, maybe just a coincidence. Figured since I had it, what the heck, wear it. But I didn't expect you to be dressed like that."

"Maybe it's that telepathy," Princess said, lightly tapping her head and turning around to the beat of the music. She waved to everyone she hadn't had a chance to speak to yet.

Christopher brought her attention back to him. "And what happened to my letter? You just now getting around to writing me, what three weeks ago, and it was only a few words. You know how I like you to write me letters . . . on paper."

"I was so busy with school, you wouldn't believe it. You have no idea what goes on up there. I'll tell you about it when I have some time."

Christopher looked at her in disbelief.

"Okay, Chris." Princess placed both her hands on his shoulders and looked him in the eyes. "I *promise* to write more often . . . and not through email."

Her promise energized him; he was on top of the world. "You like being away—"

Princess waved back at Nadira, distracting him. She was dressed as Diana Ross from the Supremes in the '60s.

The music then segued into a reggae groove and everybody went wild. Christopher responded to Princess' reluctance to slow dance and they stopped momentarily.

"You ready to eat?" Christopher asked.

"What? I couldn't wait to get back here to taste some real food, but I'm just gonna have a little something to drink for now."

Spread across the long counter was an assortment of savory foods, including buffalo wings, chicken fingers, tacos, chips and dips, chili dogs, burgers, desserts and lots of beverages. As Christopher picked up two cups of punch, three young men wearing dark glasses, ski hats, and big overcoats stepped in. Feeling uneasy, he moved closer to Princess while keeping an eye on them.

"So when you gonna invite me down there to that boarding school?"

"You don't need an invitation," she uttered, taking a quick sip of her drink. "You can come whenever you feel like it."

The three young men were making their way over from the opposite side of the room.

"Look at her," Nadira whispered to Princess from behind. "Look." Through the crowd Tamika stood with her friends, stone-faced and bitter looking.

"What's the matter with her?" asked Princess.

"I told you, she wants Christopher. You have no idea what's been going on since you left. But what I don't understand is how she gonna want somebody that don't want her, especially when she knows he wants somebody else? And she happens to be standing—"

"What you talking about now, Diva?" interrupted Jerome, coming up from behind them.

"Is that really you, Jerome?" asked Princess. "Whassup!" The two of them warmly embraced.

"How dem people treatin' you down there?"

"Pretty good. Can't complain. Look at you. The *Chili* man."

"Think my disguise is workin'?"

"If I didn't recognize you, ya know it's workin'."

Christopher took Princess by the hand and meandered through the crowded dance floor, looking for an available table. Nadira and Jerome followed them.

Once they were seated, Maverick and Alonzo joined them. Christopher noticed that the three males who were dressed as hoodlums found a table near the food. One of them immediately began stuffing his face.

"Ah yeah!" the crowd chorused, as one of their favorite rap CDs burst into the air.

"Al, who's that over there under dem hoods?" asked Jerome.

"That's just what I was thinkin'."

Jerome leaned into Christopher's ear and said, "I think that's Big Mo and his boys."

Christopher's stomach tightened and all of the evening's good feelings drained right out of him.

"See what I'm tellin' you. They're not gonna stop," Jerome said, his tone growing more insistent.

Christopher wanted to believe this was all one big coincidence. He watched them watching Deshon, who was too engaged with Vanessa to notice them. When he looked over again, one of the three men had disappeared.

"I think they ready to get busy in here, but I got something for them," Jerome uttered, getting excited.

"They might just be chillin'," Christopher said, trying to convince himself as well.

"Where you been?" asked Alonzo. "Some of them in there twenties; they don't hang with us. So why, of all places, would they want to be here, now?"

The gala mood turned tense for Christopher and his friends. Mr. McCuller moved around, conversing with the other adults present, totally oblivious to the Thugs. The first hoodlum who had disappeared returned to the table. Then the DJ mixed into an unfamiliar tune and the crowd on the floor thinned out.

"C'mon," Princess said, grabbing Christopher's hand as an offer to dance.

"No," he said sharply. "Go ahead. I'm not into that sound."

"Since when?"

The dance floor had many open areas as most of the crowd returned to their tables. "Look out there," Christopher said, managing to chuckle. "Nobody's dancing."

"So what?"

"Go 'head," he insisted, directing her to mingle elsewhere. Nadira followed her.

Watching Princess scouting the floor for a partner was demeaning. This was the first time he'd seen her since she'd left and he wanted to enjoy it. If he had it his way he would have ripped his costume off, grabbed Princess, and left the party. One of the hooded guys stopped her and Nadira as they passed him by.

"Be cool, man," Jerome warned Christopher.

"Now they're gettin' stupid."

"They want to intimidate one of us so they can jump Jerome," Al surmised.

"What they gonna do?" Maverick asked.

Jerome kept a cool demeanor and replied, "I don't know, but I'm calling my brother." He reached for his cell phone and walked over to Deshon.

"Let's break out of here," Maverick said to Alonzo.

"Why we gotta leave?" Christopher asked. "We just got here."

"Yeah, there's gonna be some bloodshed if they come my way," Alonzo grunted.

"Just be cool," directed Christopher, feeling jealous and sick to his stomach.

Jerome returned, perturbed that he couldn't get any service on his phone inside the restaurant. Deshon joined them.

"That's why I'm sayin' it's time to go," insisted Maverick. "You don't know what they got up their sleeves. This place is too small."

"Let's get outta of here," Jerome commanded, leading the group toward the door.

Christopher and Jerome were the first to shoot out of the door followed by Deshon, Maverick, and Alonzo. The hoodlums fled out right behind them, leaving the partygoers stunned.

"Hey! Mr. McCuller hollered. "What's going on!"

Christopher and Jerome ran right into the hands of three other gang members waiting outside. Christopher felt the full force of their bodies as they lunged at him. One of them thrown him up against a car and a fierce punch to his abdomen knocked out his wind. As he fell to the ground he could hear the painful moans and agonizing groaning coming from his friends as they were being punched and kicked. Piercing screams sounded above his head as he tried to cradle his body against the blows, each one making him weaker. Fighting back was impossible, and all he could think to do was to protect his head for what seemed like an eternity of blows coming at him.

Seconds later firecracker sounds exploded and the frenzied screams intensified.

"They got guns," someone yelled. "They're shootin'."

"Chris! Chris!" someone called. In his seemingly sedated state he couldn't speak at first. "C'mon, talk to me." The voice sounded familiar. He could feel a strong hand shaking his face. Another hand was feeling for a neck pulse, but he was still too weak to move. When he opened his eyes and came to full awareness, he saw Ty leaning over him, stone faced and drawn.

"You alright?"

"I'm cool," he managed to say, tasting the blood in his mouth.

"What happened?"

"Punks came at us—"

"Who?"

"Boy, you alright?" Mr. McCuller asked.

The cold wind sweeping across his face revived him. The fear in Mr. McCuller's eyes drew him back to the memory of what had occurred. His large trembling hand pulled Christopher's head forward. "My God boy, ya bleedin'. I done called the cops and Jimmy called the ambulance too!"

"No," Christopher protested. "I'm alright." He suddenly remembered Princess. "Ty, they tried to . . . they were tryin' to get wit' Princess."

"Everybody's gone now, but we'll find her." Ty held on to his friend and looked around for any more injuries to his head.

On his feet, he still felt groggy. The blood tasted like iron dripping from his mouth. "My friends, Ty—"

"They gonna be alright . . . just got a couple of bruises," Ty told him.

Mr. McCuller rushed back and placed some clean towels to his nose. "I told you them boys was up to something," he said to Jimmy. "I knew it! I couldn't see who they were but I knew they was trouble," he recalled. "My mind don't never lead me wrong."

"So y'all were gonna let them kill the boy?" Ty asked annoyed.

"It was a hundred kids in there, and by the time we could get out here they started shootin' and everybody ran off." Mr. McCullough was livid. "You take care of him. I'ma hold these other boys here until somebody can come and get them."

The street was congested with cars. Passers-by peered at them as Ty led him to the Navigator. Feeling strangely unbalanced, he looked down at his feet and realized he was missing one shoe. "Wait. My sneaker."

They looked around the ground to find it. He saw pieces of his broken crown on the sidewalk and some other stray objects, but no sneaker.

"Oh Lord! They done took the boy's shoe!" Mr. McCuller blurted out. "How these young people gonna live like this?"

Christopher wanted to do a disappearing act. The crown his mother made him was destroyed. His rare time with Princess had ended in disaster, and one of his sneakers— a brand new pair he'd just purchased—was gone. The night that had begun with great anticipation and the promise of so much fun had turned out to be an unforgettably humiliating experience.

"WHAT ARE you gettin', a .22 or a .25?" Frankie questioned Christopher, reaching into the trunk of his car parked in the alley of an old abandoned apartment building in the 'ville', short for Bedville, just south of Telham Park. He was a short white man, in his late twenties, with a droopy left eyelid and very fidgety. "Or you want to try this .45?"

"Give me the small one," Christopher decided, glancing over the selection of guns that were individually wrapped in plastic inside a microwave oven box. At 5:50 p.m. it was already pitch dark. The last encounter with the Eastern Thugs brought out a monster in him—a shadow side—that had a mind of its own.

Frankie unwrapped the .25 semi-automatic handgun and pulled it out as if it were a toy. As he snapped the parts in place, Christopher and Deshon jerked in surprise. He observed the firing mechanism and drove the clip into the chamber in one smooth maneuver. His steady hand gripped the weapon and pointed the barrel toward the ground as if he was going to fire it.

"This one can work anywhere. Your pants, your coat, or you can throw it in your bag with your books. You know how to work this thing?" he asked, passing the gun over to Christopher.

"No, but I'll learn," he replied, holding the gun with trembling hands. There was something ominous about the cold metal instrument. He admired the workmanship while Alonzo and Deshon made their purchases. With little time to ponder, Christopher made a decision and dropped the weapon in his backpack.

"Here you go," Christopher said, handing Frankie three fifty-dollar bills. He snatched them and jumped in his car without even counting them.

"Er'body straight?" Jerome asked. He was waiting at the entrance of the alley to look out for any spectators or police.

"We good," replied Deshon.

Numerous abandoned dwellings lined the streets of Bedville. It was hardcore ghetto right down to the foul stench in the air. People there were angry and volatile and would just as soon shoot you as they would greet you. Hopelessness reigned in the cold atmosphere where dreams were long abandoned, and a positive future was a shot in the dark. Residents on the barren streets were scarce this night, with the exception of small cliques of young local boys dealing drugs from their prospective enclaves.

The number 11 bus took Christopher and his friends across town back to Telham Park. Possessing their weapons, they walked with cocky attitudes, superficially empowering them.

"Let's go to my house," offered Jerome.

"Nah, let's go to my basement," insisted Deshon. "My people ain't there."

Christopher had no opinion and remained quiet as his conscience began working on him. *I'm carrying the instrument that could drain the life out of a man. An element that has turned good communities to treacherous battlefields and city parks to cemeteries.* He thought about his mother, but foremost on his mind was his father, wondering how he would react if he had knowledge of this.

"You aiight?" Jerome asked Christopher, hurrying through a traffic light across the boulevard.

Christopher nodded affirmatively.

"Let's get a pack and somethin' to drink," Jerome suggested, approaching a store.

"Yeah, that's good," Christopher agreed. A cigarette right about now was what he thought he needed. In his mind he could see his father's face looking drawn and solemn. But the vision was completely overshadowed by his hatred for what the Eastern Thugs had done to him at the Masquerade party.

"I'ma get somethin' to drink," Alonzo said, passing his bag to Maverick to hold. Holding an unlit cigarette, he walked in ahead of them. While making their selections, Al put a six-pack of beer on the counter with such confidence and ease, the salesman never questioned his age. He could easily pass for twenty-one and did so anytime he needed to.

Christopher felt that every adult eye was watching him as if they had X-ray vision and could see what he was carrying. The Arab man seated at the entrance seemed to peer suspiciously at him. A police car pulled up promptly as they walked out of the store. Christopher was so nervous his body went numb and he temporarily lost his sense of direction. The others didn't flinch. In fact, they didn't seem to be moved at all.

Walking, Christopher pulled on his cigarette extra hard, inhaling more smoke than he was accustomed to. It burned his throat, causing him to cough. His eyes teared up and the streets became blurred.

"Whassup wit'chu?" Deshon asked, concerned about Christopher. " 'Cause you kinda quiet."

"Just thinkin'."

"Thinkin' is right," Jerome jumped in. "I'm thinkin' on the Thugs and how they gonna be dancin' to a new rhythm when they come this way."

" 'Cause you know they're not finished," Maverick added.

"I know, but the next time's gonna be more than bullets shooting through the air," contended Jerome. "They gonna have a target. And trust me when I tell ya, somebody's gonna be running around here with a magnetic hemorrhoid."

Christopher pulled on his cigarette, more lightly this time. Memories of the aftermath of the Masquerade party appeared before him. He gritted his teeth and his veins pulsed vividly in his right temple. Never again would he bear the brunt of other people's cruelty. Ty couldn't drive him to school and pick him up forever. And if his new "investment" served him well, he wouldn't have to.

"You comin' with us?" Deshon asked. " 'Cause, yo . . . we all packin' now. Somethin' go down, you know what to do."

"Each one, hit one," they all said in unison, bumping their fists.

"Y'all go ahead. I gotta pick up my brother," Christopher said.

"Remember, yo, we ain't tryin' to get caught with this steel," said Alonzo. "It's for protection only. So keep it on the DL unless you want to be doin' some time."

"Negative," muttered Jerome, shuffling from side to side. "We ain't tryin' to hear dat."

"That's what I said," agreed Deshon.

"My brother never got caught with his," Jerome told them, "and he schooled me not to claim it if I ever do get caught. It's not mines. I found it."

"I already know that," said Maverick. "Just don't get caught with it smokin'."

Christopher stood motionless as a strong surge of wind brushed up against all of them.

"Only problem is, we can't carry them to school," Alonzo said, looking at Jerome.

"We gotta be able to have them in school just like anywhere else, 'cause they tryin' to get us in there, too. What if that dude would have got to one of us in school that day and we wasn't prepared?"

"Yeah, but we can't get 'em past the metal detectors," Maverick pointed out.

"No, you gotta get 'em through the bars," said Jerome.

"The bars?" everyone said at once, looking perplexed.

"Ya'll don't know about the bars?" Jerome asked.

None of them were familiar.

"Look, if you go through the lunchroom, all the way to the end, you'll see that staircase that's right behind the kitchen," Jerome explained. "You don't want to walk up the stairs. You go around to the back of the staircase. Right there you'll see the big window with these metal bars, but you know they're always locked. Now there's a corner at the bottom of the bar that's been bent in. It's just big enough to stick your arm through and pull up the window. One of us can be on the other side and we can put that joint in one bag and slide it through the space, a piece at a time."

"I know where das at," Deshon said, passing his Vaseline balm over his lips.

"We can't do that every day," said Maverick.

"Why not?" asked Jerome. "We just got to meet up somewhere at the same time every morning to do it."

"I'm wid it," Deshon consented.

"We don't have to take 'em with us every day, we can leave 'em in the lockers, know what I'm sayin'," suggested Maverick.

"Then what's the point of having them if you're gonna leave them at school?" asked Jerome. "We might leave 'em on the wrong day and something go down in the streets. Or what if security decides to do a random check on the lockers and find 'em?"

Everyone agreeably dismissed that idea altogether.

"It's a chance either way," Christopher said.

They stopped at the corner of the boulevard before parting company.

"Let's meet at the bagel shop in the morning, like 7:50," Jerome proposed.

"Why we gonna meet so early?" asked Maverick. "Classes don't start until eight-twenty."

"Yeah, and you used to coming in at 9:00," said Al.

"Get yourself up early and be there," Deshon told Maverick.

"And if somebody ain't comin' to school, let one of us know," said Jerome, addressing all of them.

"I'm out, yo," Christopher said. He shook hands with each one of them. As he turned and walked away, he said, "Early."

six

On payday Christopher gave thanks. Money in his pocket confirmed his understanding in the cosmic law of attraction. Focus on the things that you want, work for it, and create your own reality. He wanted to become great at manifesting money; it felt empowering and 'money answereth all things' according to biblical scripture—material things, anyway. After picking Joshua up at Lou Lou's, they headed toward the boulevard to see what was available in the stores.

Their divided interests led them in two different directions. Joshua's stricken gaze rested on the GameBoy in the electronics store, while Christopher went into the florist's. Peeling off several dollars, Christopher deliberated between the purple or white dendrobium orchids, his mother's favorite. "Two bunches please," he told the sales clerk.

Two doors down, with his finger pressed against the glass, Joshua had a smile on his face so wide he glowed. "Look! It's got the bigger screen and it lights up. You gonna buy it for me?"

"Uh . . . what I told you? We can go half and half or I'll pay for it up front, but you got to pay me back. How much you got?" The words flowed from Christopher as if they had been extracted verbatim from his father's own lips. He'd drilled those principles into Christopher's head, repeating them over and over to him when he was a child.

Joshua's face turned serious. "I saved um . . . seventy-two dollars and seventeen cents."

"Okay, the price is one ninety-nine, do the math."

As Joshua thought about it, he looked up and locked eyes with the man standing behind Christopher. He inched closer to his brother, a sibling instinct, and asked, "Who's that?"

When Christopher turned around, two men with almost the same build, wearing bomber jackets, turned and walked away. "I don't know."

"They were lookin' at you like they was 'bout to do somethin'."

"Ain't nothin' to dat, li'l man," Christopher chuckled nervously, his instincts now on full alert. "Let's get out of here."

"What about the MP3 player?"

"We can look at it another time," Christopher said, looking in every direction. "Time to take you home."

FIRST ON Christopher's list of priorities, once in the house, was to secure his weapon. In his room he removed the gun from his bag, wrapped it in a hand towel and eased it inside one his sneakers and slid the shoebox underneath his bed.

Christopher moved into the kitchen, listening as Gilroy began playing a string of melodic combinations in different musical styles. He started dinner and logged onto the Internet where he found an email from Princess, and for a few brief moments he forgot all his troubles.

To: Christopher Murphy" <lightningspeed@blackfolk.com>
From: "Princess Brixton" <pbrixton@boraviacollege.com>
Subject: Keeping In Touch

Dear Christopher,

Comment ca va mon ami? That's French for how are you doing my friend? You had me worried for a minute but I'm glad we had a chance to talk before I left. What a welcome home surprise. Too much idle time up there. Unlike here, where it's never a minute to waste so that kind of trouble doesn't exist. Don't give into the drama. Keep your eyes on the prize. By the way, Grandma appreciates you visiting and helping her out. So do I.

Hey, I had the strangest dream about you. You were running around the track and all these people were chasing you, but no one could catch you. Eventually you disappeared and somebody found your clothes and sneakers, but you weren't in them. What do you make of that? You know me. I'm always dreaming about something.

I'm doing a research paper in history on ancient civilization. I think I want to focus on the pyramids. Got some info for me? References? Holla Back! ASAP!

-Buttah

Christopher immediately responded:

To: "Princess Brixton" <pbrixton@boraviacollege.com>
From: Christopher Murphy" <lightningspeed@blackfolk.com
Subject: Research Reply

Buttah, Buttah, what's going on? You know how to make a dude smile. Good to know you're still thinking about me. You looked so good that night I wanted to kidnap you. Everything here is stable. I'm working more hours at the shop to make some extra loot. Funny you had that dream because the coach is still stressing me.

You want to do something on ancient civilization? Write about the mysteries of the building of the pyramids. As tall as they are, weighing six million tons or better, no one can logically explain how the Egyptians did it. Do you know why they're shaped liked that? Perfectly aligned, true to North, South, East, West, positioning—- Okay, nix that Buttah, you didn't ask for a lesson. You know I get carried away with history but that's some mad engineering genius, don't you think? If you want, you can do a comparison of scholarly theories. All of them have different explanations about how they were built, but none of them hold true because if anybody ever figured it out, they'd be making pyramids all day long.

If you want, you can research the history of civilization. Some scholars tried to make the claim that Egyptians were not African people. Make an argument for that. What you can do also, if you want, is tell the story of how Africans migrated from Ethiopia to the Middle East and began intermarrying and all that. There's a lot of info on this. Northeast Africa is where Jesus traveled, so that tells you where it all began. If you need some references, I can talk to Elias down at The Book Mart.

You still sweet? Need anything? When are you coming back to me? You want to hear some of my creative writing? Check this out. It was a blinding winter snowstorm, high up in the mountains. Big white flakes fell lazily from the gloomy sky silencing the town. You could hear the snow being crushed beneath your footsteps walking. Despite the cold, my soul burned a feverish flame as I made my way to the royal cabin where my Princess awaited. Give me your honest opinion. Don't be too honest. Peace.

FlightRisk

Christopher's focus was disturbed at the succession of doorbell rings. "See who it is, Josh," he said, reviewing his message before sending it. He leaned back and clasped his hands behind his head.

"Every time I go to the door there's nobody there," said Joshua, appearing in the bedroom doorway.

"Um hum," Christopher said absently, engrossed in his reading.

"Somebody keep ringing the bell," Joshua whined, "but nobody's there when I answer it."

Christopher looked up suddenly. At the same time Gilroy changed his soft melody to an improvisation of flatted notes, blues-style. He revisited the terrifying scene, a distraught and beaten Santos whimpering like a child saying, *"Somebody rang the bell. I answered, but nobody was there."*

Christopher leaped from his seat, reached underneath his bed and pulled out his sneaker.

As he headed toward the door, Joshua trailed closely behind him. "Whatchu doin'?" he asked.

"Go finish doing your homework," he replied quietly. "And from now on, when the bell rings or somebody knocks, you call me. Don't answer that door any more!"

Joshua sensed his brother's anxiety and followed his instruction.

Around seven o'clock, keys rattled in the door, and Joshua jumped up. "That's Mommy."

Relieved, Christopher rushed into his room, put the sneaker back in its place and got to the door just in time to greet his mother.

THINGS WERE going according to plan at school. Each day Christopher and his friends met early, smuggled their bags through the window and traveled closely at all times. Strangely, all the incidences of violence seemed to have ceased since they'd purchased their weapons. Maverick contended it was the quiet before the storm. Alonzo said he found out that the man who sold them their weapons also sold them to the Eastern Thugs, so they probably knew they were armed. Jerome urged the rest of the group to become members of the Dark Shadows because he felt they were going to need the protection. It was only a matter of time.

THE NEXT WEEK, on an uneventful Tuesday, Christopher, Deshon, Jerome, Maverick, and Alonzo decided they'd had enough education for the day. After fourth period they cut out of school to hang out with Jerome's brother Rob at Doobey's house.

The McGrady Houses was the oldest of the projects on the South Side of Telham Park and, by any standard, the worst: graffiti was everywhere, only one elevator was working and there was the sharp odor of urine in the stairwells.

The peephole on apartment 14D was old and rusty, and the bottom of the door was bent as if someone had tried to kick it in. The doorbell echoed into the deep acoustics of the hallway, as Jerome laid on it several times.

A bright-eyed young woman with naturally kinky hair—between eighteen to twenty, dark and appealing—opened the door wearing an all-black, one-piece spandex suit without shoes. She was short, with breasts as big as volleyballs and a curvaceous, protruding backside. "Whassup," she said, looking them all over with a dismissive glance while leading them in.

Lingering above the fragrant incense was the smell of fried chicken. Two young men were seated in the living room, where Christopher, Alonzo, and Maverick joined them. Jerome and Deshon went into the kitchen.

"Ayyyy, what up my people?" greeted Rob, wearing a doo-rag on his head. "Y'all just in time." He had a toothpick in his mouth and was holding a blunt in one hand, a bottle of champagne in the other.

"Lightning, whatchu been up to?" he asked, embracing him warmly. "Ain't seen you in a minute."

"Makin' it do what it do. You know how it is."

"I feel you."

"Ay, there's buckets of chicken in there," announced Jerome, who had already been in the kitchen and was eating a drumstick. "Help yourself."

Loading up their plates with chicken, biscuits and sides, they gathered around the table. The two guys seated in the living room exchanged a few words with each other and then walked out. Rob popped open a bottle of champagne and set a tower of plastic cups before them. He filled each cup to the top. Unaccustomed to the etiquette of drinking the expensive beverage, they swigged it down quickly as a thirst quencher.

The food hit the spot. Each one of them, except Maverick, had a cigarette lit. In no time they were feeling lightheaded watching a music video when the doorbell suddenly rang. Vanessa entered the room carrying a big plastic bag from the 99 cents store. Christopher couldn't see what Deshon saw in her besides her well-toned body. To him, Vanessa's attractiveness was obscured by her over-flirtatious manner. She was loose, generous with herself, and had a big mouth just like her mother.

"Hello," she said to everyone and followed Deshon to the back.

Rob poured more champagne and their heads began to mellow. Christopher took notice this time of its dry, bland taste and how it foamed on his tongue before he swallowed it.

"Dat one right there, yo, das hot," said Doobey, joining them in the living room. He slipped in as quiet as a thief, an occupational habit for the tall, lean stalwart. At twenty-two, he didn't believe in working—legitimate work, that is—but he wore the best of everything. Judging from the rings on his fingers and the diamonds in his watch, he was making not good, but excellent money, in some kind of way.

Everyone's attention was now directed to the soulful, sultry movements of a new R&B artist called Nakitah.

"Yo, das the one from Kentucky," said Alonzo.

"Kentucky?" Doobey drew his head back. "Shooot. Let me find out they got shorties down there lookin' like that. I might have ta relocate."

"She workin' it," agreed Jerome.

"The Thugs got beat down yesterday, you heard?" Doobey said to Jerome.

"My brutha told me."

"I heard y'all took 'em down with pipes and chains," recapped Alonzo.

Rob sucked his teeth and then dug in between them with the toothpick. "They got off easy."

"Where were y'all?" Christopher asked.

"Makin' my rounds on the South Side, over there by Leeky Street," Rob replied. "They were over there with their boys. Then they gonna ride up on me like some cowboys.

Yeah," he frowned at the impossibility of their plan, "like I was stupid enough to be out there by myself—"

The building in the movie blew up in flames, diverting everyone's attention. "Whoa, ho, that's what I'm talkin' about!" Rob exclaimed, but then picked up where he left off. "Thugs came up on me telling me to move. Randy and nem was watchin' the whole thing. They started musclin' on me tryin' to get me in that trunk. Stupid, yo, they didn't know the Shadows was gonna wash them."

The more Rob sipped on the champagne, the more animated his moves became. "My boy Rahkim had this pipe wrapped in a burgundy towel, right. So the dude didn't see it comin' and out of nowhere, *Ka Piya!* Whacked him ova da head." Rob's bulging eyes made them all laugh. "Dat joka was shocked still, yo . . . eyes glazin' like he just took a hit of crack." As he laughed, it was easy to see Jerome's resemblance to him.

The doorbell rang again. Doobey passed a serious glance to Jerome. "Take them to the back," he instructed.

Maverick, Alonzo, and Christopher followed Jerome down the hall, past a bathroom and a closed door. Rob's best friend Jah sat in a high-back leather chair behind a wooden desk, talking on the telephone. Christopher had heard of the man but this was his first time meeting him. He was dark and gruesome-looking with cloudy red eyes, a gold eyetooth with long, thick dreads wrapped around the top of his head. Jah nodded, acknowledging their presence.

Christopher was drawn to the unobstructed view of the South Side of Telham Park and the distant city skyline. It looked dull and gray, like the color of guilt. Stroking his chin easily, he felt like he was dreaming. Shortly thereafter, Doobey came into the bedroom and removed a safety deposit box from the desk drawer. Inside Christopher saw little square manila envelopes, several small brown paper bags rolled up, and fat wads of money wrapped in rubber bands. No one flinched as they scoped what was going on.

Christopher turned back toward the window and stared out. The cityscape was avalanched by images of chaos: drugs, violence, poverty, and despair—all adding up to an inescapable trap. His father used to tell him that ever since the days of prohibition, alcohol, drugs, and number running had become organized crime activities, and that gangsters would always be among the people. The casualties of these nefarious operations—the uneducated, the poor and the powerless—would be permanently ensnared.

"We get 'em on the South Side 'cause that's where all the action is," Jah explained. Maverick, Alonzo, and Jerome huddled around him, listening hungrily to his every word about battling the Eastern Thugs for territory. "It's more money there than you can count. That's why we got to build up the numbers 'cause they got more than us right now, but we got the other goods to keep them off us. See, if you want to get—"

"Want some more?" Deshon offered, entering the room with a fresh bottle of champagne. He was tight-faced and couldn't stop talking. Christopher knew him well and it was evident what he had been doing with Vanessa. He listened to his friend's gibberish as more champagne numbed his system.

The telephone, hooked up to an amplifier, rang loudly throughout the apartment. Jah sat back in his chair like a king on his throne, pinching his nose with the pad of his thumb as he talked. He alarmed everyone when he abruptly rose to his feet. The cell phone on his belt rang at the same time. "They dead! Buried! " he barked, storming about anxiously. "Where's my money? What? You tell 'em I'm comin', no betta yet, don't say nuthin." He slammed the phone down. Then reached into his drawer and took out an eight-inch silver gun, cocked it, shoved it inside the front of his pants, and tore out of the room, talking as he walked. "They got Nacho and Tommy!" Christopher heard Jah say. "They hurt, yo! Bad. And the cops got 'em. Call Muscles and Ray Ray."

They all looked at each other blankly, shock and alarm slowly pulling them out of their champagne haze. Jerome walked out and joined his brother in the living room.

"What's going on?" Vanessa asked, coming out of the other room.

"Somethin' happened to Nacho and Tee," Deshon answered.

"Like what?"

"Finish them!" Doobey commanded, diverting everyone's attention down the hall. "And I want them cemented!" Maverick looked at Deshon and then at Christopher in a dumbstruck gaze. Alonzo's face wasn't readable. He always appeared that way.

"We down wit it too," Jerome declared, stepping back into the room.

"What happened?" asked Deshon.

"Retaliation, yo. They just told Jah the Shadows got their faces busted. Nacho got his teeth knocked out and some ribs broken. On top of that, Tommy got robbed."

Jah and Rob spewed bitter anger, calling other members for help. A universe of coldness reared up on Jerome's face. "We traveling, yo. What y'all gonna do?"

"Let's do it," Alonzo said.

Inebriated from the champagne, Christopher had the ego of Goliath. Before he knew it, and against his better judgment, he was teaming up with the rest of the group.

Muscles, Ray Ray and two other guys must have been close by. They appeared at the door in no time.

"Take the car," Jah said to Rob, handing him a set of keys. "I'm going to the hospital." He swept past them, furious yet determined, and together they all stampeded down the stairwell.

There wasn't a hint of sun in the afternoon sky as they all spilled out into the street. Jerome sat in the front of the older model Cadillac with his brother Rob. Christopher was huddled in the back seat with Alonzo, Maverick, and Deshon leaning horizontally across them. In search of the Thugs, Rob drove around the North Side first, through the boulevard, by McCuller's, and then around the school. Christopher could see Coach Lappatina on the field with a small group of track athletes.

Back on the South Side, Rob trailed around the projects and the nearby abandoned streets that were reputed to be Thug territory. This went on for an hour. Christopher kept watching the car clock. He was scheduled to be at work in less than two hours.

"They hidin', yo," said Alonzo.

"They know the Dark Shadows is on 'em," said Jerome.

"Then they should be more than happy to meet our acquaintance," stated Rob, in a tone so menacing it sliced the air.

"They scared—like roaches," Deshon said, "and they're all somewhere together."

"Let's smoke 'em out," suggested Maverick.

"With what?" Christopher asked. "What you think this is?"

"We can do some stink bombs, or Molotovs," Maverick rambled off.

"You stupid!" said Alonzo. "Like they're just sittin' somewhere waitin' for us to find 'em."

Christopher sat there, among a group of young men conspiring to hurt other young men for the sake of egos, drugs, and territory—and he realized they were dead serious. The moment was surreal, as if he were coming and going, in and out of his champagne high. They drove around the precinct, the park, the Laundromat, the pizza place. They checked clothing stores and even boutiques, hoping to find at least one. No sign of the Thugs. At the end of a long narrow street on the border of the South Side was a corner store called Big Boy's Deli.

"I'ma get somethin' to drink," said Jerome, getting out.

"I'll get it," volunteered Deshon, "'cause that was my last cigarette and I need to stretch. Y'all want somethin'?"

So caught up in the adventure, everyone said no. As they waited, few words were exchanged. Their heads bobbed to the hard-core rhythm of hip-hop music on the radio.

Soon Deshon rushed out of the store and opened the car door, reaching for his bag. "Give me my steel!" he shouted. "I'ma do him the same favor he did me."

"Who's in there?" asked Rob, eyeballing the front of the store.

"The one that put that knife in my shoulder!"

"He by hisself?" asked Jerome.

"I don't know if he is or not, but I'm gonna get 'im."

"Let's get out," Jerome said, turning to his friends in the back seat.

Christopher's heart was pounding hard and erratically.

"There dey go!" shouted Rob.

Two guys, one whom Christopher recognized, glanced at the car and took off running.

"Get in," yelled Rob. He put his foot to the pedal hard and the car screeched as it raced off. He chased after them, almost colliding with another vehicle. Then the two Thugs split up and ran on opposite sides of the streets, throwing Rob off momentarily.

"Get that one in the black," Jerome said, directing his brother to make a right turn. The Thug's hoodie came off, clearly exposing his profile.

Rob stayed on his trail as he dodged through cars like a scared animal. He cornered the street where alternate side parking was in effect and the Thug could only run on one side. Deshon clumsily cocked his gun and fired two shots that sounded like an explosion. The slim figure ducked, as agile as a rabbit.

"Get that punk!" shouted Jerome.

"Whassup wit'chu now?" yelled Deshon. He aimed at the darting figure and fired another shot.

At the corner the Thug turned into a dead-end street and meandered through the parked cars. No one could spot him. Then, just as they thought they had him cornered, he came up behind them and returned the fire. The bullet flew right above the car, scaring Christopher to death. "Move out!" he yelled.

The Thug suddenly surfaced from behind a car and ran the opposite way. "There he go!" said Rob. Jerome fired out of the window as Rob turned the car around. There were no people in sight on the street, but they heard a woman's screams in the distance.

"Move out now!" Christopher charged. He was adamant this time.

Maverick was scared, too. "We need to break out," he said, his voice wavering with fear.

Rob seemed oblivious to their words and continued with his manhunt, watching everything that moved. Christopher's inclination was to jump out and detach himself from the madness. He feared the bullet that might kill him and leave his mother and brother to face the world alone. He yearned for his father to magically remove him from the massive chaos. Christopher rose up and reached for the door. Two more shots fired out, causing all of them to duck, but it was unclear where they came from.

"Don't get out!" ordered Alonzo.

"Then move!" shouted Christopher. "Move out, now!"

Deshon fired once more in the air as Rob sped off fast.

"Punks," Jerome lamented. "I almost had that one. He was gonna feel the fire."

The occupants of the car were overcome by a stinging silence as they drove back toward the north side of Telham Park. The repercussions of what had happened began to settle within all of them, and their tension thickened the air inside the car.

Back in the neighborhood, construction work slowed traffic to a complete stop along Merle Street. An update on the presidential campaign trail was being announced when Rob changed the channel.

Out of nowhere, a black Navigator pulled up beside them and Ty jumped out. He opened the back door, eyeballed each of them and fixed his angry eyes on Christopher. "Get out!"

All eyes turned to Christopher, who was too shocked to speak. Ty snatched him out of the vehicle by his collar, opened the passenger door of his Navigator and pushed him in. To escape the gridlock, Ty backed up on the sidewalk of the one-way street and moved into the stream of intersecting traffic.

"So, you want to play gangsta."

Comment or question, Christopher couldn't tell the difference. He trembled inside, reviewing what had just occurred. Ty drove to a nearby industrial area next to the bread factory. These desolate streets came alive at night where an unlimited amount of drugs were sold and prostitutes solicited business. Right now, it was quiet and there wasn't a soul to be found. Ty came to a short stop, exited the vehicle and opened Christopher's door. "Get out!"

Christopher moved cautiously and for the first time he could see a hint of the streets in Ty; he had the finesse of a fox. "You wanna be gangsta, right?" he asked, grabbing him by the shoulders and forcing him up against the vehicle.

Christopher looked away to escape the heat of Ty's gaze. That's when Ty pushed him against the vehicle with a force that made Christopher quiver. "School's not good enough for you . . . 'cause you gangsta now."

"Thhhat's not true," Christopher stammered, feeling compelled to say something.

"When you're ridin' in a car with gangs and they got guns and drugs and enemies, what do you call that?"

"But I wasn't shootin', it was—"

Before Christopher could finish the sentence Ty's heavy hand came across his head with a smack that distorted his reality, temporarily blinding him. He had a guilty man's reaction—weak and wobbly.

"How many times do I have to tell you? A split-second can ruin you! What would have happened if the cops would have run up on you?"

"But I didn't do nothin'. They were the ones—"

Another smack to the side of his head came quickly, nearly causing Christopher to stumble. "No, not *they*. All a y'all would have been charged with possession of a weapon. Were there any drugs in the car?"

"No," Christopher nodded slowly. His head was still throbbing.

"Rob was in the car. How do you know what he had?"

The look on Christopher's face must have betrayed his naiveté. "I…I don't—"

"Know what 'not knowing' is gonna get you?"

"No."

"Possession of a weapon, drug possession, conspiracy, and attempted murder, that's what."

"But I didn't do nothin', I was just there."

"Did you hear what I just said?" Ty squinted incredulously, inching closer to Christopher. He seemed to be growing bigger with his anger.

"Um, yeah."

"That makes you an accessory! Now I know you know what that is."

It just occurred to Christopher that Ty had witnessed the exchange or in some way found out what had happened.

"They didn't hit nobody."

"Not this time they didn't, but you would've still been facing possession charges if you had been caught. That's a minimum mandatory sentence of three years in prison—automatically! What's wrong with you, man?"

Christopher could feel the water building in the corners of his eyes. Beside his ego being bruised, Ty's hand hurt something fierce.

"I thought you were better than this!" Ty admonished, his face crumbling with disappointment.

Christopher shook his head, denying the accusation.

"A split-second is all it takes. Their life, your life, prison, pick your tragedy. Either way, you finished! Your father is turning over looking at you." As Ty spoke, Christopher saw the corners of his mouth turn down in disgust.

"Why you not in school anyway? I gotta come check on you every day and make sure you're not cuttin' out. I can't believe you." He grabbed him up by the shoulders and pressed his brawny massiveness against Christopher, forcing him back against the Navigator. "Don't be so quick to jump in a car with a gangsta," Ty warned in a low voice.

"Uh huh."

"They might have drugs and guns in their possession that you don't even know about. And God forbid somebody gets shot or dies. Nobody's gonna believe you're innocent. You're gonna be doin' time right along with them and now you got a record—for life. You want that?" Ty backed off and turned away, staring into the distance.

Finally, Ty turned back to him. "Get in the truck." He spoke kindly, as if nothing had ever happened.

Ty drove up the Biltmore Parkway and passed three exits. As they approached the bifurcated road, there stood a blue bus with white lettering that read "Eastern Region Correctional Facility." Next to it were a group of men, mostly Black and a few Hispanic, bent over, diligently picking up trash. Their neon-orange work clothes were apparent underneath their navy blue pea coats. Ty slowed the vehicle to a crawl as they passed by.

"This is what you get for good behavior: a day out in the cold to dig ditches or pick up other people's garbage,"

Ty stated with the certainty of a man who's been there. "Nothing like the smell of fresh air, some sun on your back and a look at the new cars swishing past you . . . driven by people free to come and go as they please. 'Specially when you know those cars gonna be obsolete by the time you're able to buy one—if ever."

Christopher could see a certain yearning in their desperate eyes when they looked up, regret resting heavily on their tired backs.

"Your father would be real proud to know the life you chose for yourself."

The inmates were soon out of sight, but the picture stayed with Christopher.

"What do you think any one of them would do to be in your position right now?" Ty asked. "Free to do anything you want to do. Be anything you want to be. A gifted athlete, who can outrun everybody…."

Victor was outside talking to a customer when Ty drove up to Magic Auto Center. "See the money you make here," Ty said, directing his eyes toward the establishment, "You can't make that locked up. When you work in prison, a good job pays you five dollars a day, and they work you like a mule. Want to buy a car? Invest in some stocks? Buy yourself some nice things? No such options there."

Christopher had never heard Ty speak like this before. Deeply ashamed, he wanted to tell Ty the truth about the gun and his fear of the Thugs. "I wanna apologize—"

"You can make one mistake, you're entitled," Ty explained, cutting Christopher off in mid-sentence. "But if I catch you out there like that ever again I'm gonna leave you there 'cause I gotta do me. Understand?"

"Yes," Christopher nodded.

"How many times I told you prison is no place for a man to be?" Ty continued, steeped in a steady calm. "This ain't television you watchin'. You associate with gangstas . . . that's what you become. But I'm not going down with a sinking ship."

Victor came over and spoke briefly with Ty as Christopher exited the vehicle. The thought of his boss hearing the news disturbed him terribly. Later on, he expected Victor to confront him about what had happened. But he didn't, because Ty never said a word.

seven

"Tomorrow's Thursday already," Christopher realized. The week had passed so quickly that he had barely done anything to prepare himself for an upcoming English exam. Sitting in the living room, Christopher perused his notes while he watched *Modern Marvels: Then and Now* on The History Channel. Between the phone calls that had interrupted him, helping Joshua with his long division, and preparing dinner, he had retained very little of what he had studied.

At seven-twenty he heard the locks on the door unbolting. Mrs. Murphy walked straight into the kitchen, a scowl fixed on her face and sat down at the table.

"What's the matter, Mom?"

"If it's not one thing, it's another," she replied glumly. "Just when you think …"

Gilroy's trumpet played an erratic medley with piping sharp notes and thick, dull flats and then eased into a fragile tone.

"What's wrong?" Christopher asked, disturbed by her subdued mood. "Somethin' happened at work?"

"Is this what I'm sending you to school to do?" she asked placing an open envelope on the table. "Make C's and D's?" His mother was a stickler for report card dates and had asked to see it every day this week. With so many things occupying Christopher's thoughts, he forgot to check the mail and grab it before she did.

"This is what I have to go to your school and face your teachers with?" she asked, dragging her gaze aimlessly across the room. "Especially when I know you can do better. If it's that job that's taking up all your time, it's got to—"

"No, Ma, it's not that."

"Well what is it?" Mrs. Murphy charged, her face greatly troubled. "Tell me something because I don't understand. Look at this." She tossed the report card over to him.

Christopher didn't respond at first, staring at the rows of C's and D's. What possible explanation did he have for falling short of his responsibility to excel in school? It was his parents' bedrock principle.

"Listen, Ma," Christopher began, and then he paused, giving serious thought to his response. "Understand what I'm trying to say. School . . . it's not interesting to me. I . . . I'm not learning anything and certainly not the things that really matter."

"What kind of foolishness is this I'm hearing? What really matters then, Mr. Genius?"

"Hear me on this," he pleaded softly. "What I'm learning in . . . chemistry, geometry, history and English . . . I'm never gonna see again in my life."

"What do you mean?" His mother looked confused. "You gonna see it again in college."

"But what if I'm not planning to go to college?"

In an angry reflex his mother stood up, grabbed him by the shirt and pressed him against the wall.

"Mommy, no!" Joshua cried, looking on.

"Oh, but if you live in *this* house you're going to college, you comprehend that?"

Christopher nodded affirmatively out of sheer fear. They stared eye to eye. He was no longer her baby boy she was disciplining. He was a young man evolving into adulthood who thought he was ready to take on the world, even though she knew he was at the initial stage of self-discovery. She suddenly yearned to go back in time when Christopher was young, her husband was alive, and things were simpler. Quelling the tension, she eased away from him and decided to allow him the space for some intelligent dialogue.

"So, tell me about this great big plan of yours."

"Look, Ma, if college is gonna be just a higher level of high school, then what's that gonna do for me? They don't teach me nothin' about—"

"They don't teach me '*anything*,'" Mrs. Murphy interrupted, correcting his English. "If you paid more attention to your studies, your language skills would improve."

Christopher took a deep breath and allowed a brief pause to come between them. "Okay, Ma, how important is language when you're a Black man in America? Come on, racism is alive and kicking with its own legs, and all the proper language in the world won't change that. I mean, look . . . we're not even included in the history books like we should be. Daddy used to talk about it all the time and nothing's changed. We talk about Martin Luther King on his birthday and a few others during Black History Month and that's it. I get tired of hearing about Lincoln freeing the slaves and reading their version of American history—which only tells us we were slaves. What about *our* history, *our* stories? Look at the things we built in this country . . . with our labor, with our genius. If Daddy hadn't schooled me on my history—where I come from and all the things that we've done—I wouldn't know. I gotta read about the African Burial Grounds in the newspaper or see it on TV, or else I'd be like my friends . . . lost. I'm not feeling it, Ma."

"I understand what you're saying and you're right. Sure, this society would have us believe we evolved from monkeys, became slaves, and were the footstools to everybody else. But c'mon, look at your ancestors and the people before you. They didn't accept it, which is why you have the opportunities you have today. And Rosa Parks, Bill Cosby, Oprah and Dr. Ben, uh Benjamin Carson—they didn't accept it, either. You can't expect an institution like a public school to teach you about your history. Remember, we were never intended to be educated in the first place. And before integration, we only received a tiny portion of what white folks were getting. Nobody ever expected us to accept the hand we were dealt—and win!

This is a new day. You've got technology and computers. There's no discrimination on the Internet. An African American man is our president—never thought I'd see the day. But he surely wouldn't be there if he had your attitude. Look . . . the idea is to learn all you can from school and then make your decision. That public school education, the one that you don't want, can get you a scholarship to college, and from there you can do anything."

"But Ma, people are making all kinds of money out there and they didn't go to school. You see how those rappers are living?"

"We can't be a race of people rapping, Son. What's the significance in that? It might make you feel good, yeah . . . make you rock 'til you drop, but c'mon. We've gotta a whole generation out there competing for a record deal. I see them . . . thirty and forty years old, like there's nothing else to aspire to."

Christopher lowered his eyes, pondering her words.

"I see you doing great, significant things, Son. Because to whom much is given, much is required. I tell you that all the time. God didn't put us all here to be musicians and athletes. We're mathematicians, engineers, scientists, and physicists too. That's the real legacy. So while your little generation is so consumed with money, music, and all this material stuff, you're missing the big picture. That's a part of the brainwash, too. Throw them a couple of rap deals, a car or some bling-bling and they'll degrade their women all day long. Forget about the real issues at hand. And then what makes it so bad is, even with the money, what are they doing with it?"

"I'm not saying I want to live like that either, Ma, I know better but look at Ty. He's got his own business and he's making more money than people who work every day. He dropped out of school and earned his degree later."

"Yes, he did and that's good, but he had to do it behind bars!"

"I'm not saying I want to go that route, but I'm not going to conform and be another robot out there doing what I'm told to do."

"Well now, that sounds real good coming from somebody who doesn't see the value in his education," she said, raising up and clasping her hands together. "You're gonna always work hard, even when you have your own business. But when you're educated you can chose your work, and not allow it to choose you. Don't you see? That's the real freedom. Then you can strive for excellence. Be married to it, eat, sleep, and breathe it until you become the best."

With words as biting as Mr. Murphy's would have been, Christopher knew his mother was right. He wanted to yield to her plea but was caught between the snare of his own ambition.

"Son, I've lived almost four decades before you were even born, and I've seen some things that you wouldn't believe. You see these varicose veins in the back of my legs, boy?" She stood up and slid her skirt above her knee.

Christopher stared in another direction, avoiding her suggestion.

"Look at them!" she insisted.

Nothing could break him down more completely like viewing the evidence of his mother's trials, the network of blue veins resulting from all her hard labor.

"I have them because I didn't go beyond high school. I had to content myself with stressful labor because I didn't make smart choices. I cleaned toilets and washed floors in some of these big companies when I could have been using my head. Now look at me today—still working with my hands. Your father was determined to have his own business one day. That's why he worked so hard—high blood pressure and all. He wanted more for himself, more for *you* and *Joshua* particularly. It took a heart attack to stop him."

Christopher stiffened his body and clenched his teeth to fight the tears building up in him.

"Son, I'm not saying this system is right, because there's a lot of wrong all over the world. But education is where it starts. It'll be your compass, giving you direction . . . and you can accomplish anything. I don't care that you have a great love for cars. If that's your passion, go for it. But with education you can manufacture your own cars, with *your* name on them! You don't like the history you're being taught in school, build your own institution. You may not have been born rich, but you have a wealth of important qualities that your father and I instilled in you. Understand what I'm saying?"

"Yes."

"Your father's not here any more and I can't teach you how to be a man, but we have to work with what we've got."

His mother heaved an exhausted sigh and set her gaze on the report card. "There are people out there who wish they could learn," she continued softly. "Here you have it all and you want to gamble with your fortune. And then God smiled upon you with an extra blessing. Son, you can run. With that alone, you can get a scholarship into college. Personally, I couldn't care less about you being an athlete, but if it opens a door to something greater, then do it." Mrs. Murphy's face began to cave in like she was going to cry, but she didn't. "I didn't raise any criminals, and one day I would surely like to see some scholars coming from this family. Make up your mind, son . . . while you're young."

His mother's lackluster eyes rendered not only parental defeat, but also the sadness of a lonely woman. "You've been smoking," she uttered quietly. "Think I don't smell it on you? I don't say anything because I want you to come to your own conclusions. That's how you learn. And how do you think I feel when you come home beat up . . . and then you try to hide it? Then you lost the crown I made you…."

Christopher lost the battle to restrain his emotions when he locked eyes with his mother's crestfallen gaze. Gilroy's dramatic tune washed over the air, adding a new layer of poignancy and melancholy to the moment. Mrs. Murphy slid the report card across the table and walked to her room, leaving a visible trail of disappointment for Christopher to navigate through. That was worse than her screaming, her wailing, or any punishment she could have ever given him.

eight

C'mon, five more, you can do it. Four, three . . . Deriving no pleasure from his strenuous workout routine in Goodman's Gym, Christopher mentally encouraged himself with positive thinking. His friends were with him.

"I'm gonna do some arms today," Maverick said, who was spotting someone.

"I'm a try to go into the ring," said Alonzo, now in his fifth set of dips.

"Do what you want, but I'm going to Doobey's," said Deshon. He had just completed his last set of pushups and paused to admire his pumped muscles in the mirror. "Y'all wid it?"

"Let's go see the fight first," suggested Jerome, curling twenty five-pound dumbbells.

"Yeah, I want to see my man," Alonzo said. "He killed 'em last week."

"Jarrod's out there?" asked Maverick.

"I don't know," replied Jerome, returning the weights to the rack. "But I saw Marcus and Tremaine when I came in."

Christopher wasn't going anywhere near Doobey's, but he never missed an opportunity to see champions at the peak of physical fitness, training to fight. "Alright, let's get to the ring," he agreed.

The ceiling fan circulated hot air in the boxing area, providing little relief to the pungent muskiness. But the motivation behind the unpleasant scent of stress release, muscle-building and burning fat was priceless to the young men—a sort of soothing to their inner angst as tightfisted blows sank into punching bags. Jump ropes whistled through the air.

"No pain, no gain," Alonzo said as they circled the ring. Marcus, the six-foot-three, two hundred-thirty-pound fighter, was in the ring viciously sparring with an unknown opponent. At nineteen, Marcus was one of the strongest guys Christopher had ever witnessed in a local ring. The brown-skinned heavyweight with shoulder-length dreads was solid muscle and had fists like cement. Unlike other neighborhood fighters, he didn't entertain spectators with a showboat style or fancy footwork, displaying quick moves and jabs. He simply targeted his position on the opponent, found his opportunity and knocked him out.

Vigorous breaths flew out of the boxer's lungs as they sparred in the humid air. Jerome looked around for Old Man Stevens, who ran the gym. He was ready to put on the gloves and spar with Alonzo.

"Give me your money," a husky voice bellowed, grabbing Jerome's neck from behind.

Christopher turned around and saw Kadeem, a mobile entrepreneur offering designer originals at inexpensive prices.

"I saw you coming," Jerome responded casually. " Whas cookin', Money?"

"What y'all up to?" asked Kadeem, a reddish-brown man who had the good looks of a model. In his early thirties, he still had the slender build of a boy.

"Workin' out, just like you," Jerome answered.

"Yeah, we want to be just like you when we grow up," Christopher said.

"Handsome and intelligent?"

"No, a balla wit' deep pockets," replied Deshon, shaking his hand.

"Whatchu got today?" Maverick asked, looking down into Kadeem's duffel bag.

When Kadeem wasn't working for the post office he was at the gym, or selling his goods at one of several places around Telham Park where large crowds gathered. With a slippery grin that could con even the greatest of cons, and the courteous manner of a prince, Kadeem could sell anything.

"I got some long-sleeved jerseys, casual velour warm-ups. Oh, and I got some mock-neck sweaters. Look at these—a hunit percent cashmere—all colors, all sizes, fifty dollars—just for you."

"What!" Jerome exclaimed. "You robbin' me."

"Whatchu mean? That's not even half of what you paid for the sneakers you're wearing, and I don't see you hasslin' the sneaker companies. Whatever they ask, you pay it. So why you hasslin' me? I gotta eat, too."

"But you ain't paying nothin' for this stuff, so why you charging me so much?"

Kadeem laughed at Jerome's ignorance or innocence, whichever way one chose to look at it. "How much you think it costs that sneaker company to make a pair of sneakers that they gettin' a hunit, hunit and fifty dollars for?"

"I say fifty. Half of what they chargin' me," Jerome answered with a distinct cockiness as if he were certain his response was accurate.

"No," Kadeem said, shaking his head vigorously. "Only a fraction of that. With the volume they do, the cost could come down to three or four dollars. Now look at me, I buy wholesale, but I can only buy a few pieces at a time, so I gotta pay much more than they do. You know, the more you buy the cheaper it is. When you're a lone ranger like myself, you can't buy this stuff in big quantities. Right now, I pay close to retail. Ain't but so much I can raise my prices 'cause I'll lose the support, and people won't buy it. My mark-up from what I pay is only thirty-five percent." He had them all captivated by his lesson on wholesale and retail pricing.

"You got to come by when you selling somethin' I need," said Alonzo. "You got the hook up, get me a Blackberry."

"You don't even have a job. What do you need with a Blackberry?"

"I gotta communicate with my boyz," Alonzo explained, pointing to all of them. "And my shorties, yo."

Kadeem couldn't resist laughing. "Nah, I can't do that. You don't need any more distraction. You're too young."

"What, for a cell phone?" Jerome looked awkwardly at Kadeem. "Why you so serious man, we can handle it."

Kadeem knew the history of Jerome's brother and the kind of lifestyle he lived. "You ought to be spending your money on books, a computer or something. Take a trip and see the world. And I got some nice sweaters for you to travel with."

A burst of laughter exploded near the entrance, causing everyone in the gym to turn and look. Christopher recognized Darryl. Beside him were Big Mo and three other Eastern Thugs. Their laughter ceased. In the light, their faces could be seen clearly. One of them gestured with a head motion toward Christopher and his friends.

"Come check on us when you got something we need," Jerome said.

Vibing on the exchange between the two, Kadeem said, "Ignore them. They're just more distraction."

Solid stares between the men declared a challenge, and the talking ceased. The blows to the punching bags were swift and consistent.

"And what's that gonna do?" said Kadeem. "Whole lot of other ways to vent your frustration."

"Yo, yo, yo," a wolfish voice sounded out. "What's up, Tee?" A big man dressed in black appeared behind the Thugs.

"Guess you ain't goin' nowhere tonight." Maverick uttered sarcastically to Christopher. "Your bodyguard is here."

Ty could be specter-like sometimes, appearing when Christopher least expected him to. Christopher's friends dispersed like guilty men when Ty approached them.

Together, the two of them worked out on the machines, doing trapezoids, deltoids, biceps and triceps. Then they moved to the punching bag, where Ty showed him how to use it as a form of exercise. When they finished, Ty rented two sets of gloves and walked them over to the ring. "We got next."

"We who?" Christopher asked. The thought of being on the receiving end of one of Ty's iron fists was not a pleasant one.

"You and me, that's who," Ty replied, watching Marcus bear down on his new opponent. He had been going strong for more than twenty-five minutes.

When Marcus's sparring partner received a terrifying blow to his face, he decided that he had had enough.

"C'mon, it's me and you," Ty said, leading them into the ring.

"Why don't you spar with Marcus?"

"Nah, I want you. Besides, I might hurt Marcus."

Christopher swallowed hard and felt a knot in his stomach as the other men took notice of them. The Thugs were still lingering and all his friends stopped their activities to observe Christopher and Ty.

"Don't worry about them," Ty said, his uncanny sensitivity to others' feelings sharply on point. "Just do what I tell you to do." They threw up their hands and began shuffling around the ring. "Never take your eyes off of me."

"Alright."

"Now come at me however you want and I'm gonna block you."

Christopher threw multiple punches at Ty before he landed one to the side of the head.

"That was soft," Ty critiqued. "You can do better than that."

They continued to shuffle and try to land punches. Christopher's gloves were becoming heavier. Then Ty threw one punch and Christopher skillfully dodged it.

"Good," said Ty, never taking his eyes off Christopher. "You gotta be quick. You gotta anticipate my moves. Now give me some real power on that punch."

Christopher summoned all of his strength. He jabbed and punched while keeping his eyes glued to Ty's.

"Much better," Ty commended. They continued to spar, both of them breathing heavily. Ty caught Christopher with a punch or two, but they both knew he was going easy on him. In quick sequences Christopher threw short, stabbing punches back at Ty.

"Good, good!" Ty praised. "But you gotta plant your feet and punch with your whole body, not just your hands."

Christopher exercised his neck, jerking it from side to side and followed Ty's direction. He moved strategically and threw jolting punches. He could feel the increased force behind the blows as he lunged forward.

Ty wore a shrewd smile as he worked Christopher all over the ring. "Punch with power, baby, and move like lightning."

Christopher looked good to the spectators and he knew it. Ty began dodging blows and throwing some. Christopher was returning them blow for blow. For a short time it felt as if they were really boxing. After twelve more minutes of fast and furious action Ty decided to stop. "Alright, you had enough for today."

"Where you off to?" Christopher asked Ty as they left the locker room.

"Gotta make a few runs. You got a minute?"

"Yeah."

"Take this ride with me."

"Ayo, I'm out." Christopher told his friends as he and Ty headed to the street. He felt rejuvenated after the boxing workout and the steamy shower.

"So what's goin' on, young man?"

"Not much."

"Things coolin' down?"

"Seems like it," Christopher replied, getting into the Navigator.

"You didn't go to work today?"

"Nah, I'm taking Wednesdays off now."

"For what?"

"Neede some time for myself."

"Hangin' out with that group? That's not time alone."

"They're my friends, and they like to work out, too."

"I never took you to be a smoker," Ty said, changing the subject. Thought you were smarter than that."

Coming from Ty, those words stung Christopher. Not only could Ty see everything, but he had a keen nose, too. "It's just somethin' to do when I'm with my friends. I mean, I don't buy no packs or nothin'."

"Well, if that's what your so-called friends are indulging in, they're not the kind of people you need to be with."

"Yeah, but they're my friends."

"Friends?" Ty grunted. "One day you'll see who your friends really are. C'mon man, you bigger than that. At least *I* know you are, but *you* got to know you are."

Christopher changed the radio station and turned up the volume slightly. "Where we headed?"

"I gotta check on somebody. Oh yeah—" Ty paused slightly, remembering something. "You got plans Saturday morning?"

"Not really."

"I need some help moving some furniture. Early."

"Alright. I'll let my mother know."

When they passed the old Horizon Motel that had been turned into a shelter for the homeless and displaced families, Christopher looked on curiously. Groups of men congregated outside the building, smoking.

"Look at them," Ty said, slowing down, pointing toward the center. "You know who that is, right?"

"The weed creed?"

"They're Thugs."

"What are they doing over here?"

"Some of 'em live there."

"In the shelter?"

"Yeah. You didn't know that?"

"Nah."

"Some of them come out of foster homes . . . been abused . . . livin' on the streets with nothing to eat. That's why they're mad at the world. Life ain't been far. But that's what makes them dangerous. 'Cause they have nothin' to lose. See that one with the black bandana, leather coat, standing to the far right?"

"Yeah."

"Been in and out of jail since he was nine. Got four kids . . . by four different women. Can you imagine *that* being somebody's father?"

"Nope."

"So what kind of chance do you think his kids will have? Look at 'em. Living in poverty . . . ain't no joke, man. Betta count your blessings." A short pause ensued. "Deep down inside . . . they're nothing but scared little boys, thugs who need some hugs.'"

Christopher had never looked upon the Thugs as the sons of mothers, or as brothers and fathers with issues, cares, and concerns like other people. He only thought of them as radical gangsters with no conscious.

"I heard they were poppin' people in Springdale now," Ty told him.

"You mean they're moving outside of Telham Park?"

"Yeah, but that's gonna be a short run. You think they're gonna terrorize the suburbs where people making money live? Them folks ain't havin' that. They'll make an example out of one of them real quick and the game is over."

"Yeah, that's right."

"See, the thing about bangers in the hood is . . . they really believe that life starts and ends there. You hear them talkin' about 'these streets is this or that and it's real out here,' as if they can't get up and move to another borough, another state. Shoot, get out the country; it's a big world out there. You think the likes of dem guys gonna come lookin' for you in Alaska or some exotic island? Most of them can't even read a map."

"That's real," Christopher agreed, rocking to the bass line of the music.

"Had any more problems with them?"

"Not since the party."

"That's whassup. I don't want to have to get with them jokas."

"I'll be alright, I can protect myself," Christopher said confidently, thinking about the weapon he'd purchased.

The neighborhood gradually changed as they drove deeper into Sagnolia Hills, two towns over from Telham Park. Pedestrian traffic had virtually disappeared. The streets were well-paved, smooth and clean. Stately, detached homes with beautifully tended lawns stood in back of white sidewalks. "One more stop and I'll take you home."

"You get around everywhere, Ty."

"Got to, if you're gonna make anything happen."

Christopher looked over at Ty's wrist. "I like that watch."

"This is an old classic," he replied, glancing at it.

"Where'd you get it from?"

"I bought this in the city."

"I never saw you wearing any thing like that before," Christopher said, observing the gold hands on the black face with the single centered diamond.

"I used to have boxes of that stuff back in the day. Seems stupid to me now."

"You startin' to sound like my pops."

Ty chuckled, reminiscing. "Mr. Murphy used to tell me I looked like a slave wearing all those chains around my neck. Then he said I had the mentality of one for buying it in the first place."

They laughed heartily at the familiar words.

" 'Let me school you, Son,' " Ty growled, mimicking James Murphy. "Then he would break it down, talking about the whole apartheid movement in South Africa and the schemes behind the diamond trade. 'Our people dyin' over natural resources growing in their country and you're supporting them.' I mean he would give you the economic principle, the players, the politics and er'thang. Spoke about Mandela like he was his blood brother."

"Yep, yep, that's my pops talkin'." Christopher could almost hear his father lecturing. "So what did you do with all your jewelry?"

"Sold some. Pawned some when I needed bail money. What I had left I keep in my box at home."

"I don't know too many brothers got that kind of gold that wouldn't be wearing it."

"Yeah, but what does it mean?"

Christopher paused in search of a response. "Means you . . . you got it going on."

"Got it going on like how?"

"You know, doin' your thing."

"You mean like I have a business, making decent money and this is what I do with it, or like I'm a hustler or drug dealer showing off in the hood?"

"You certainly ain't that."

"Anyway you look at it, it adds up to nothing. A rich man doesn't wear his wealth on his back. Can't put on your business. Can't tie your real estate around your feet. Stocks and bonds don't come in small, medium and large. Besides, the real wealth comes from within . . . and if that's intact, you're always gonna make money."

Ty's words rang crystal clear with Christopher. *What do material things really mean?* Simultaneously, he bounced his head to the sound of a rapper called Tawon, talking about the conditions of the hood.

At the next light Ty stopped and continued. "And then you gotta be mindful of the ignorant man, because for every man that's enlightened you got millions who are in the dark. That jewelry's not worth losing your life over. Plus, you'll learn as you're climbing, never let the left hand know what the right hand is doing. As far as anybody else is concerned, I'll always be a hard-workin' brother. When I start making some real money, I'll be that same brother and the quiet millionaire next door."

"I hear that," Christopher responded, nodding appreciatively.

Soon, they drove into a circular driveway leading to a two-story colonial house. When the motion sensors turned on the lights, Christopher could see a late-model Mercedes Benz parked in the driveway.

"Who do you know over here, Ty?"

"A good friend of mine lives here."

"Your friend must be doing good."

"Doin' alright," Ty said and pulled the keys out of the ignition. "Come on, let's go." Acknowledging Christopher's full bag he said, "What you got in there?"

"Uh . . . just a lotta books."

One of the most gorgeous creatures he'd ever laid eyes on opened the door. "Hey baby," she said, leaning into Ty's embrace. Smelling good, she was a slender-figured nutmeg goddess with long, pretty hair.

"Pamela, this is my little brother Christopher, the one I always talk about."

"Finally, I get a chance to meet you," she said, smiling, reaching for his hand. Her big, brown eyes mesmerized him and he could feel her sensuous aura through the softness of her touch. "Come on in."

The interior of the home was as lovely as she was—beautiful and elegant. A two-story entrance foyer with marble floors opened up into other areas of the home.

"Have a seat, sweetie," she offered as they entered the spacious living room. It was a den of periwinkle paired with white and purple pleasures.

"You hungry?" Ty asked when he and Pamela went into the kitchen.

"No, thank you, I'm good."

"Sure?"

"Yes."

"Want something to drink?"

"No thanks."

Christopher heard feminine giggling answered by Ty's hearty laughter in the kitchen. Christopher never knew Ty to be playful and humorous. Viewing the six o'clock news reminded him of the time. He could make it home just before his mother got there. She was picking up Spanish food for dinner tonight, at Christopher's expense.

The laughter in the kitchen diminished to soft murmuring. Christopher smiled to himself, feeling privileged that Ty would invite him into his personal world. To him, it was a sign that their relationship was still intact and all was forgiven.

His hand massaged his bag, and he could feel the weapon. It was time to find a safe place to put it. He wanted to confide in Ty but couldn't bring himself to. Ty might get angry, tell his mother, Victor, or even worse, come down physically on him. Possessing a weapon imposed a realm of secrecy that erected walls between him and the people he loved. It didn't feel right.

"Let's go, man," Ty said, entering the room. Next to him was Pamela with a smile spread over her gorgeous face from ear to ear. Christopher's appreciation for her stunning beauty was obvious in the way he stared at her. "What's the matter?" Ty asked, laughing.

It was impossible for Christopher to expose his true thoughts. "You have a beautiful home," he replied, with a compliment instead.

"Well, thank you. And you have to come and visit more often."

Christopher flashed her a shy smile and said, "I think I will," and they parted company.

"That's your girlfriend?" Christopher asked as they entered the vehicle.

"We're just getting to know each other."

"Man!"

Ty released a big laugh, sensing what Christopher was thinking.

"I've never seen you with a woman. No, yes I did. You used to see Karla in the building next to mine—"

"Karla? Shoot . . . that was back in my running days. Couldn't keep up with the girls, I had so many. But after I did that piece of time, all that changed." He put the keys in the ignition and stared out toward Pamela's house. "After a while all that running gets old. Nothin' good comes out of it anyway."

Ty navigated the SUV slowly out of the driveway. "The whole time I was locked up, I wanted that special somebody . . . you know, a woman I could relate to, write to or visit me sometimes. That's when you come to realize the value of a relationship. Well, some of us do."

"Yeah."

"When you become a man and realize how precious life is, you get an urge to find that better half . . . one that can be all things to you. Know what I mean?"

"Uh huh," Christopher nodded, thinking of Princess.

"That's why you want to get married when you find her. Grow together, build together, and hopefully raise a big ol' family full of knuckleheads like yourself." Ty, in a rare playful mood, slapped Christopher's knee as he turned the corner, leading them out of the residential serenity. "Give them all the things they need to survive in this vicious world so they don't wind up like me."

"You doin' good, man."

"I'm not sayin' I'm the worst man out there, and better than a whole lot of them that I know, but I'll put it this way: If I had it to do all over again I would do things a lot differently. I'd stay in school, for one; it gives you the tools you need to take on everything else."

"Why'd you drop out?"

" 'Cause I was a knucklehead. Stupid. Mad at the world."

"Mad about what?"

"Life. There was no money . . . my father was gone. Lot of my boys went to prison. Some of 'em got killed. And the ones that were left were strung out."

"So why didn't you go back?"

"By then, I was in the streets. Making that fast money, you think that's all there is 'cause that's what the hood teaches you. See where it got me, right?"

Ty's words bounced around in Christopher's mind, giving him much to think about. When they reached the corner of the building, Christopher could see Pop-Pop walking aimlessly down the street, wearing only his sweater and pants. "Ty, let me out here, man. I gotta get Pop-Pop back inside. He needs to be dressed warmer than that."

"Alright. Take care of yourself," Ty said, gripping Christopher's hand.

"I will. You too."

"One."

The old man walked right into Christopher and didn't recognize him. "Pop-Pop. Where you goin'?"

"To the community center. They havin' dinner for the seniors."

"Okay. You can go, but you need to put on some heavier clothes. It's cold out here."

The old man's mind had a tendency to drift in and out. Christopher buttoned his sweater and led him back home. As they walked, Christopher looked down at Pop-Pop's feet and realized he was wearing two different shoes.

Back at their building, Gilroy's music was vibrating throughout the first floor.

"Who dat?" Pop-Pop asked. "Gillespie . . . or Parker?"

"Pop-Pop, it sounds like them, but that's Gilroy."

"Gilroy who?"

"Our friend on the second floor."

"Oh, oh, oh."

There wasn't much to Pop-Pop's small, one-bedroom apartment. His lifestyle had taken a downward spiral since his wife had passed away some five years before. No one ever thought he'd live to be eighty-eight without her. Christopher remembered how he and his wife used to baby-sit for him when he was a child. They were gentle, patient, and never too strict.

Among the clutter, Christopher managed to find the appropriate clothes and a match to his shoe. "Okay, Pop-Pop, we gotta get you a coat."

"Don't worry, I got it," he insisted, pulling his classic wool field coat out of the closet. For a small man, Pop-Pop was very strong. He had worked hard in his day and his hands felt like a worn baseball glove.

"Want me to walk you to the center?"

"Sho'. I could use the company."

"Okay then, just wait here. I got to go pick up Joshua. I'll be right back."

Joshua asked a million questions on the way from Lou's Lou's to their house.

"Here, take my bag," Christopher told Joshua as he opened their apartment door. I'll be back in a few. I gotta walk Pop-Pop somewhere. Ay, start doing your homework."

"I can use your calculator?"

"Yeah."

Pop-Pop talked every step of the way, telling tales from decades ago. Never was any detail of his life spoken of without his beloved Clarice. In his mind, she was still with him.

When they reached the corner of the Straton Community Center, Christopher pulled Pop-Pop away from the curb when a passenger van filled with children swerved around the corner. A terrible thought suddenly struck Christopher as he heard their laughter.

I didn't put the gun away. Joshua's got my bag and I left him in the house alone.

Christopher nearly dragged Pop-Pop into the community center and then blazed through the streets of Telham Park, trying to get back home. He recalled giving Joshua permission to use the calculator in his bag, which made him run faster. Explosive gunshots went off like crackling thunder in his mind. Images of Joshua lying in a pool of blood, fighting for his life. He could see his mother fainting, distraught and grief-stricken.

"No!" he pleaded. "No God, please!" These ugly thoughts put fire underneath his feet and caused him to run recklessly. Swerving between pedestrians and jumping between car bumpers, he made all kinds of promises to God about the gun if He spared Joshua. The encroaching grief sank deeper and his heart hammered, anticipating the tragedy in his head. His legs expanded like rubber bands as he tore through the apartment building, leaping up the steps three at a time to get to his brother.

Christopher banged hard as he nervously fidgeted to fit the key in the door. "Josh!" he called frantically, jerking the doorknob. "Josh, open the door!" There was no answer. Fumbling, the keys fell out of his hand. His fists pounded the metal door as a flash of Joshua lying dead in a pool of blood revisited him. "Josh! Josh! Open the door," he cried. There was still no response. In a fit of rage, he rammed his body into the door with such force he chipped the paint inside the frame and the hinges loosened. With the back of his foot he kicked the door with all his strength. "Open the door, Josh!" Frantic, he picked up his keys and tried again. Christopher could hear the neighbors opening their doors as he finally drove the correct key into each of the locks. Suddenly, the door flew open and Joshua jumped out of the way of its force. There he was, standing and breathing, his pants dangling around his knees, his eyes bulging with fear.

"What's the matter? What happened?"

Christopher was so grateful to see his brother; he fell to his knees, grabbed him by the collar, hugging him close. "What took you so long to answer the door? I was calling you."

"I was on the toilet," Joshua mumbled. Christopher held onto Joshua so tight, he muffled his words. "I wasn't gonna open the door at first 'cause you told me not to answer it. But when I knew it was you I kept saying 'Wait a minute! Wait a minute!'"

"But I couldn't hear you, li'l man."

"That's 'cause you was banging on the door so hard."

"Okay, you right, alright." Releasing his grip, Joshua's innocent eyes pierced Christopher's heart. "Sorry 'bout that," Christopher said, standing up and feeling the relief of what felt like five hundred pounds lift off his back. "Go back to the bathroom and handle your business, man."

After securing the locks, Christopher leaned his perspiring body against the door, thinking. *God is merciful. Again.*

Despite being drained, he was grateful to be able to do ordinary things like homework, cleaning up the house, doing the dishes, and awaiting his mother's arrival, versus dealing with the tragedy he knew he could have faced. In return, he made a promise to himself to get rid of the gun as soon as possible.

"A MEETING with the debate team?" asked Mrs. Murphy entering the house the next evening. "Since when are you—"

"Jordon's been on my back for the longest," Christopher explained, "and I told him I would come check 'em out before the next competition."

"Oh, so you're giving some thought to—"

"I'm not sayin' I'm ready to become a member, but if I can help them out—"

"What about dinner?"

"I'll grab something later, Ma," he replied dashing down the stairs. "I'm already runnin' late." Attending a debate team meeting wasn't a far departure from the truth, technically, since Christopher had every intention of honoring his word, only it wouldn't be taking place at this particular time.

Unseasonably warm temperatures descended on Telham Park and Christopher could smell rain in the humid air. It was a long, lonely walk to the reservoir, twelve blocks in all. As if in a dream, people appeared out of nowhere, walking and whispering, as he offered his thoughts to the rippling stream that ran just below the road. He thought especially about his father, remembering that he had taught him how to ride a bike in that very same area, first with training wheels, then without them. Only a superman like his father—it seemed—could run as fast as he could ride, then turn back to a mortal man and quietly feed the pigeons. The roar of a jet airliner overhead stole his attention and soon drowned out his sweet memories prompting him to move to the reservoir's far side.

Alone, with the sky blanketing him and a partial moon glowing, he took the gun out of his pocket. 'Trouble no more,' he chanted in his head. Then, with all his might, he tossed it over the fence. The moment the gun pierced the water, Christopher felt a huge relief.

The sidewalk broadened as he started walking back, and so did his thinking. *I'm actually a perfect fit for the debate team, Dad. Got all the right characteristics. I'm well read on social issues, politics, historical perspectives and religion. I certainly know how to listen. I'm open minded and I certainly have patience. The research I don't mind but then I gotta deal with—"*

Then, out of nowhere, a bright light gleaming next to him caught his attention. Two young men jumped out of a four-door car with tinted windows startling Christopher.

"Whatchu up to?" the taller one asked, sounding almost friendly.

"Nothin'," he replied, tossing glances between the two familiar faces.

The shorter one's smile slid into a cunning frown. "But we think you are," he said.

"C'mon, I'm tryin' to do me," Christopher said, attempting to reason with them.

The lights of the car beamed stronger as it inched toward him and panic gripped him. Acting on instinct, Christopher shot out into the street, crossed to the other side, and began running in the opposite direction. The driver turned the car around and caught up to Christopher. When he saw this, it shocked him into another gear. He sped up and turned into the next block. It was a U-shaped, one-way road that looped clear around from the adjacent street. Christopher tried to cross to the other side when, all of a sudden, he saw the car again. The driver was coming down the one-way street after him.

In his haste to escape, Christopher ducked behind a car, thinking. Running around the loop would be the perfect opportunity to get caught, as it was the obvious way out.

He couldn't backtrack and go out the way he came in, because he knew he could run into them, and the thought of that sent him into a frenzy. Someone was coming out of a building and closed the door, and the only way to get in was by intercom. He couldn't blend in with the group of ladies he saw from afar getting out of their car. Something occurred to him as he ran alongside the building that led to the back of the garage. No entrance there. He came back out to the street, walking cautiously, watching for anything that moved. Just as he cornered the loop, two of them came rushing up on him like mad bulls.

Christopher conjured up every bit of speed he had in him and flew down the dark street. He dodged between two parked cars and when it was safe, he ran across the street. Then he faked them out and crossed back over to the other side again, finding temporary refuge between the bumpers of a Jeep and a car. He crouched low to the ground like an alley cat. The fender of the Jeep sat high above the curb, allowing him to see any foot movement or vehicles rushing by. As if by divine intervention, he heard a voice whisper the command: *Lie down.* His body relaxed as he flattened his back on the ground and slid completely underneath the Jeep like Victor had shown him. Only this time he did it without the creeper. His sense of hearing, now as sharp as an animal's, was on full alert. As he lay still, he could hear their voices nearing.

"You see 'im?" one of them said.

"Nah," the other one replied, "But he's gotta be over here. There's only one way out."

"He might've cut through the back."

"Check around those cars, yo."

Christopher lay there in silent trauma as their voices grew distant. He didn't move a muscle. He saw a black cat dart out from a car across the street. *Please don't let that cat come over here.* With pressure mounting he only allowed his mind to focus in one direction—returning home to his family in one piece. The Thugs passed by him at least three times before they finally gave up.

The house was quiet when Christopher returned home. His mother and brother were each in their rooms. In his paranoia, and still rattled by the evening's events, he couldn't focus on much of anything. He sat back on the living room sofa and watched a PBS segment on *The Man Who Killed President Kennedy.*

Christopher had hoped that discarding the gun would bring him peace. Instead he was facing more terror than ever. Things were spiraling out of control and he had to do something, and do it quick.

nine

Alonzo was the last one to join the troubled group at lunch time the next day. They discovered the school had repaired the window cage, making it impossible to smuggle in the guns. Neither of them had anticipated a problem, and there was no alternative plan set in place. Jerome decided to skip school and take all the weapons to his house and they would meet up with him later.

"Man, we shoulda all went home," said Alonzo shaking up his chocolate milk.

"And then what?" asked Maverick. "Can't cut out every day. We just gotta find another way to pack 'em."

"Jacked up my plans," Deshon lashed out. "I'm supposed to be meetin' Vanessa."

"We got other issues," remarked Alonzo. "That's the only protection we got."

"Nah, sorry dudes, that's not workin'," Christopher spoke up. "My brother could've been killed."

"You losin' it!" criticized Deshon, slamming his fist into his other hand.

"I did what I had to do."

"But you didn't have to throw the piece away," said Alonzo.

"Why you ain't call me?" Maverick asked. "They prowlin' around everywhere. I coulda used another one."

"So we sit around waitin' for 'em until they catch one or all of us?" asked Christopher. "And then what? This one shoot that one. I'm not livin' like that, and I'm not risking having a gun around my little brother, yo. I told you." Disgusted, Christopher looked away and then turned back. "I'll take a bullet before I see him take one."

"Just gotta be more careful where you hide it," advised Alonzo.

"Did you hear what I . . . so if he should find it I gotta dead brother and then I'm going to jail. Think this is a game?"

"But you could have sold it," persisted Maverick. "That piece costs some dough."

"I don't care about no money, yo."

"That's on you," said Alonzo, "but they come after me like that—"

"All this fight we got in us, let's press our weight against some real issues, man. Fight for some reparations, the Rockefeller Drug Law, boycott the companies we makin' rich when we don't get our justice. Anything but this! We look stupid fighting each other."

"Yo, I'm outta here after sixth," Deshon said, changing the subject. He had no regard for what he deemed Christopher's flimsy rhetoric. "This girl keeps texting me with messages from Vanessa," he mumbled looking at his phone. "She gonna meet me at Doobey's so you know what that means."

"So what you gonna do?" Maverick asked Christopher. It was as if the depth of his words had flown right over his head.

"I'ma live."

"Ya hope." Deshon said in a low voice, cutting his eyes over at Christopher.

"Huh," Christopher grunted. "We tough, yeah, but what are we changin'? People dyin' in the world, oppressed and starving, and this is all we do?"

"I ain't tryin' to hear dat!" Deshon spewed. He passed a Vaseline balm swiftly over his lips and stood up. The diamond cross around his neck gleamed especially bright against his mustard shirt. "I ain't tryin' to save the world, I'm lookin' out for me." Pointing to his wounded shoulder he added, "This is what I'm fighting for. You betta come back to reality, yo, and stop being a punk!"

"Ever known me to be a punk?"

"Today you are. We got a job to do and you—"

"Then do it!" Christopher exclaimed. "But I'm not wid it."

Deshon looked puzzled. "Where you at, yo? Can't never find you when it comes down to gettin' the job done."

Christopher resented Deshon's words and cut his eyes toward him.

"Whatchu gonna do, yo?" Alonzo asked.

Christopher could tell Alonzo was at least attempting to consider his reasoning. "I'ma go to some people that can do somethin' about it."

"You gonna tell your Moms?" asked Maverick.

Christopher disregarded his ignorance. Turning toward Alonzo, he asked, "Thugs running the world now? They above the law?"

"You goin' to Ty?" Al asked.

"For starters, yeah. But whoever I talk to don't make a difference. I'm doing what I have to do."

"And whatchu think you gonna do, reason with 'em?" Deshon retorted. "Thugs don't know nothin' about that."

"That's the problem. They don't have nothin' to lose. That's what makes 'em so dangerous. Brothers like that disguise their suicide as homicide, 'cause deep down is nothin' but a death wish."

"Oh, so you're gonna teach them somethin'?" Deshon shot back coldly.

"I'm not teachin' 'em anything, but they'll understand me when I'm done."

"You might be dead by then," Maverick uttered.

Deshon checked the time on his Sidekick. "You losin' it, yo. All them books you readin' got you stupid."

"Yeah, okay."

"The real men got a job to do," hailed Deshon.

"Shut up with that nonsense," Christopher said. "Y'all ain't no real ballaz."

"I wasn't speakin' to you . . . punk!"

"Punk ain't got no scars, and a nut for a brain."

The words were barely out of Christopher's mouth when Deshon lunged at him, knocking him off balance. He tried to act like he was playing, but the force behind his push said otherwise.

"That's all you got?" Christopher challenged.

"My tricks ain't for no kids, yo."

Christopher attempted to leave when Deshon wrapped his arm around Christopher from behind, putting him into a chokehold.

"You supposed to be musclin' me or somethin'?" asked Christopher, feeling the pressure.

"I thought we was cool but you leavin' me out there." Deshon's voice turned husky through his rapid breathing.

"Lemme go," Christopher demanded as Deshon tried to drag him. Christopher resisted his force with a quick elbow to his stomach, causing Deshon to loosen his grip.

In seconds they had wrestled down to the floor with Christopher at the advantage. He had a clear shot to hit his face, or his shoulder where he had been cut. Exercising self-restraint instead, Christopher wrestled with him until Maverick and Al pulled them apart. They had the attention of half the lunchroom now as well as two security officers running toward them.

"What's the problem?" the officer asked, glancing from one young man to another. "Not you two."

"It ain't nuthin!" Alonzo declared, forcing a chuckle. He and Maverick backed Deshon away from the crowd, hoping to avoid any disciplinary action. "They just flexin'."

"That's not allowed here," the other officer chided. "You know the rules."

"You alright?" the first officer asked Christopher.

"Yeah, I'm cool," he replied, smug-faced, gathering his belongings. Before he walked away he turned to

Deshon and said, "Betta slow your roll, dawg. This ain't no friendly fire."

It was then clear to Christopher that making a responsible decision would be one made alone. The thought of breaking ties with Deshon was disturbing, though the memory of the humiliation he endured at Deshon's cutting words would make it easy to drop his friendship.

I'm going to Ty's Car Wash after school, and I'm going to tell him everything.

"God loves you, Christopher," called out Nikki Walker, a member of the 'Students For Christ' group.

"I know He does," smiled Christopher. His eyes then fell upon an approaching student who seemed vaguely familiar. The way he walked, the shape of his head and his obvious avoidance of eye contact with Christopher made him stand out.

"Greater is He that is in me—" Nikki said, quoting biblical scripture and placing a religious pamphlet in his hand.

"...Than He who is in the world," Christopher continued absent-mindedly. He looked down at the pamphlet, titled *GOD is Good*, and then shifted his eyes up quickly to get a closer look at the approaching youth. But by this time he had disappeared.

AKILA BARKSDALE sat down next to Christopher in seventh period English. She was a good friend of Vanessa's.

"I thought you would be hanging with your girl today," said Christopher.

"Who, Vanessa?" she questioned, copying the "Do Now" assignment.

"Yeah."

"No, she went to Manhattan with Nakima. Her cousin's 'spose to be doing some video."

Christopher paused at her words. Vanessa was supposed to meet Deshon at Doobey's. At least that's what somebody texted Deshon and told him.

Christopher stared at his closed notebook, his suspicions now aroused. Nakima grew up to be one of the finest looking girls in Telham Park. She was one of those girls who had been brought up strictly. Her mother never allowed her out of the house except during school, at least until things got ugly with her big brother. Cedric was running with the Uptown Boys, a drug mob, and got into trouble over some financial dispute. He began flaunting jewelry, wearing expensive clothes and throwing a lot of money around. Then he bought a new car, which he claimed was his cousin's, and people started looking for him. His mother took him down South.

The two sisters, equally gorgeous, were left behind with a cousin and began to do as they pleased. They grew up, grew out and went buck wild. Nakima started hanging out in the game room with Tommy, a known Eastern Thug from way back.

"Lemme have a coupla pages," whispered Ricky, seated across the aisle from Christopher.

Still thinking of Deshon, Christopher didn't respond.

"Yo, yo, let me get a couple of slices."

"Here you go," he uttered, looking blankly over at Ricky and handing him his whole book.

The teacher took attendance, calling names out loud. He thought about the possibility of Vanessa playing both sides of the fence, as Maverick had warned him about. Then he dismissed his suspicion. *But what if . . . Deshon would be going out there alone.*

"Ms. Cotrell," Christopher said, raising his hand abruptly. "It's an emergency. I need to use the pass." He shot out of his seat and grabbed the wooden plate before giving her a chance to respond. He walked down the third floor corridor, peeking into classroom windows looking for Deshon. Science and English classes he eliminated, and followed his mind to History. When he got to room 217, it was empty with a note on the door that read: seventh period History—Special Assembly.

When he opened the door to the auditorium, it was dark and quiet as the students watched a film. *I'll never be able to find him like this. I doubt he's in here, anyway.* Christopher used the back staircase to go down to the lunchroom.

He was stopped by security. "This isn't your lunch period."

"It's not, but I got special permission to get something to eat," Christopher lied, holding up his pass.

"What's special about you?" the female officer joked.

"Nah, I missed lunch working with my teacher."

"Okay," she said, allowing Christopher to pass.

The lunchroom had become crowded, making it more difficult to spot him. He saw Terrance and a guy named Enzo, who said he had recently seen Deshon, but no one knew his exact whereabouts. Christopher went into the bathroom, but he wasn't there either. He asked a student named Will for his cell phone. He first tried Deshon's cell. No answer. Then he called his house.

Just before he hit the exit door, a guy they called Spoonbread stopped him and said, "Lookin' for your boy. He cut out already."

"Which way he went?"

"Out the back."

"Aiight, good lookin'."

Something was wrong. Christopher could feel it. On a mission to find Deshon and warn him, he headed outside and circled the building. There was no sign of his friend but something told him to continue walking. To his surprise, more than a block from the school, sat the blue Jeep, double-parked. Christopher could see the movements of the crowd from a distance, stopping and staring.

He began jogging when he saw a group of men ganged up and ready to fight. A glimpse of a mustard-colored shirt between the huddle alarmed Christopher. Picking up his speed to a sprint, he got close enough to see Deshon being struck several times. It sent a shock wave through him as he watched his body being flung around like a rag doll.

"No! No! Get off 'im!" Christopher yelled long and hard, his adrenaline skyrocketing. He moved as fast as lightning through the echo of his own words. Blazing with repressed fury and with every ounce of strength he could muster, Christopher drove into the two young men with full force, knocking them both to the ground. He hit one of them hard, a punch to his right ear and then struck his face. Then, the second assailant grabbed him from behind and put him into a chokehold so strong Christopher gasped for breath. Refusing defeat, the wounded one squirmed out of his misery and came charging at him. Christopher braced himself against the one holding him and kicked him in the face with both feet, causing him to fall to the ground while the one holding him was knocked off balance.

Seizing the moment, Christopher reached back over his shoulder with his right hand and drove his fingers into his eyeballs. The Thug loosened his grip, enabling Christopher to elbow him in the gut. Police sirens sounded from afar as Christopher scrambled to help Deshon.

"T-Bone, we gotta go," a voice yelled from the Jeep.

Struggling, the sweaty Thug ran to the Jeep. When Christopher turned around, a gun was pointed at his chest.

"Show me what you got!" The other one challenged, inching closer to Christopher. Former spectators began to flee. When he cocked the gun, all time at that moment stood still. The wind stopped blowing. Traffic halted. All Christopher could feel was the thudding vibration of his wildly palpitating heart.

"We out, Rummy, let's go!" yelled the first Thug from the Jeep. "Cops iz on us, yo."

The Thug snapped out of his rage and glanced over toward them. Using that second of distraction, Christopher leaped toward Rummy and tackled him to the ground. He slammed Rummy's hand against the cement again and again, finally releasing it. In a surreal moment Christopher recognized him. He was one of the young men who had chased him down the dark street at the reservoir.

This Thug was going to shoot me. Sacrifice his own life just to deprive me of mine, take me away from my family, and I don't even know his name.

Like an efficient fighting machine, Christopher threw punches with both fists as hard as he could. A crazed demon had taken over him and he lunged for the Thug's neck. With both hands, he squeezed and squeezed until the Thug's eyes began to bulge, his voice cackled, and his body slowly surrendered.

Suddenly, several arms grabbed Christopher and forced him to the ground. His hands were pinned behind him and positioned for handcuffs. A hundred pictures flashed in Christopher's mind as he slowly took in the present reality.

"He's got a gun," an officer said.

"Is this yours?" another officer asked, pressing his knee against Christopher's spine and handcuffing him.

"No!" Christopher replied. "He tried to shoot me with it."

The police stood him up, affording him a quick look at his adversary. Rummy's head was bloodied, but the ugly scowl on his face was more prominent than ever. Deshon's body lay there, as still as if dead. One cop checked his vitals while the other one radioed for an ambulance.

"That's my friend. Is he breathing?"

The officer pushed him back and said, "Does he have a gun, too?"

"We don't have any guns. Deshon!" he called out. The handcuffs on him were uncomfortable and he couldn't understand why he was wearing them.

"He's gonna come around," another officer said. He was a small white man who looked almost too young to be in law enforcement. "Paramedics are on the way. So what happened here?"

The Thug had become coherent, saying, "I wanna press charges!" But no one seemed to take him seriously.

"I left school early," Christopher began explaining while three cops—that he had recognized from school—listened intently. Then came the questions.

"Are you saying the gun belongs to him?" the first officer asked, almost in a tone of disbelief.

"Yes! He was going to shoot me."

"What are you doing over here?"

"I ran outside to help my friend."

"Why aren't you both in school?"

An officer came over with the gun contained in a plastic bag. "This belong to you?"

"No. I told them what happened," Christopher said, pointing his eyes to the other officers and that's when he saw Deshon's head roll slightly to one side. Knowing that his friend was alive filled him with a momentary sense of relief.

The officers exchanged knowing glances. "Okay, let's go."

"You have the right to remain silent. Anything to say can and will be used against to in a court of law. You have the right to an attorney . . ."

Christopher fell speechless as he was led into the patrol car. He turned and looked questioningly into the eyes of the kind officer who placed his hand on the crown of his head as he stepped in. "We have to take you in and straighten this out," he uttered.

When the patrol car began to move, Christopher looked out of the window into unfamiliar eyes. Inquisitive spectators craned their necks to see him. Others gazed as if in a stupor and stared blankly. Now, as the target of unabashed finger-pointing and comments, he was mortified. *This is a bad dream.* When he leaned back, the ache of his throbbing fist reinforced his hold on reality.

The heedless and thoughtless activity of children grew distant as the police car passed through neighboring streets. Thoughts about his life raced through his mind, and in the midst of it all he heard the haunting riffs of Gilroy's trumpet echoing loudly in his head.

Christopher ached for his father. Golden memories of their happy times together appeared in his mind with astonishing clarity. Then he envisioned his father looking wounded and angry, hurling out admonishing words more punishing than ever.

I'm in this by myself. No one could save me now. Not even Ty.

He fought the tears that were stinging his eyes and buried his head in his jacket.

"You alright back there?" the kind officer asked.

"Yes."

The two police officers conversed about mundane issues: what they were going to have for dinner, vacation days, something crazy a fellow officer did, a new iPad one of them had just purchased. For them it was just a pedestrian day, routine and uneventful. For Christopher, this day divided his life into before . . . and after.

He could have been crossing the finishing line at a track competition, taking Telham Park High to the state finals. Researching the facts of a debatable issue or arguing for the team. Watching the Civil Rights classics or challenging the logic behind the Vietnam War. He could be perfecting his poetry or chatting on the Net with Princess. Watching the Knicks, a soccer game or a fight. But instead, he was in the back seat of a police car, wearing handcuffs like a criminal. He could almost see his father weeping.

ten

The 51st Precinct was on the border of neighboring Bedville and listed among those having high violent crime rates. It had a look of trouble; an institution that resisted change—and renovations, too. Inside, Christopher looked into the occupied faces of a multiracial blend of police officers, people under arrest, victims making reports, and was repulsed by a handcuffed drug addict who had puked all over himself.

I need to call my boss and tell him I'm gonna be late. Hope they let me outta here in time to pick up Joshua and be home by seven. It's all Christopher could think about watching the big clock in front of him before he fixed his eyes on a dingy pastel blue wall decorated with photos of men and woman who were wanted and a "Guns for Cash" ad. Christopher thought he recognized one of the men but was soon distracted by a an older Hispanic woman coming out of a side room yelling and screaming about her money being stolen—in English and Spanish.

It had been a long time since Christopher's mother had been contacted at work about an emergency. When the company's automated system reported a twelve-minute wait, Christopher gave the Sergeant Ty's cell phone number, which rang into his voice mail. If he was at work and busy, it could be some time before he called in for his messages. After several attempts, the officer decided to wait as his attention was called to other matters. One phone call he received—in particular—led to a conference with the Lieutenant and it seemed to change the officer's disposition.

Christopher was uncuffed and moved to a small room with a six-by-three-foot table, four metal chairs and a clock on the wall. All the noise from the outside ceased and he was left alone with nothing but his thoughts.

Massaging his aching hand, now slightly swollen, he shuddered in fear. *What are they gonna charge me with?* He knew possession of a weapon carried a minimum mandatory three-year sentence. Six hundred and twenty-seven dollars was all the money he possessed and he needed an attorney. The extra money his mother had from monthly social security checks was being saved for Christopher and Joshua's college funds.

His hand throbbed something terrible, but not as deeply as his heart. He wished Ty had hit him a few more times, maybe knocking some common sense into him. Then he wouldn't be staring at the barren walls around him. The thought of the troubles ahead exhausted him and he slowly surrendered to the emerging fatigue.

Strangely, the tender memories of his life drew up vividly. He remembered the comfortable bed that his parents had provided for him. They would tuck him in at night and his mother would throw the sheet high up in the air and let it fall loosely like the wind. The cool sheet feathered his body like grass. Then there was the excitement he felt when his father's face appeared at the classroom door when school had ended.

Growing more tired, Christopher's head fell into his folded arms. He could hear his stomach growling, though food was the farthest thing from his mind. Lightheaded and exhausted, he surrendered to his heavy eyelids. A shimmery blur swept him to a region reaching out across the miles. He drifted further . . . and further . . . and further . . .

Eleanor Murphy and Ty stormed into the dark room marked Private Counsel. Beneath the glare of the overhead light, Christopher leaned sideways as she inched toward him, her fiery eyes burning in fury. "You're just determined to disobey me, right?" Her words echoed in his inner ear as he fastened his frightened gaze onto hers. "All the times I told you. I warned you. I pleaded with you. Don't go out there and get into trouble. I don't want the police calling me because I didn't raise any criminals," she spewed, slamming her slender hand down so hard the table rattled. Then she began pacing the room from wall to wall, indicating her displeasure and shouting imprecations.

Ty stood by the door, not uttering a word.

"I'm not getting put out on the street to bail you out because you don't want to use the sense God gave you. No, uh uh. Your brother and I still have to live, you hear me?"

Christopher was scared stiff.

"You ignoring me?"

Before Christopher could respond, Eleanor Murphy raised her hand like she was going to strike him, but she didn't. Like a woman gone mad, she paced and she talked. She paced and she reasoned.

"What are you trying to do to me, boy?" she asked desperately, flying back over to Christopher. Then she launched into an episode of senseless laughter. Her rising voice sliced through the air and filled the room with false amusement. Then she heaved and sighed, heaved and sighed. Growing tired, the merriment dissipated. Tears slid down her face and she began wailing in grief. "How could you do this to me?" she cried. "How could you do this to your father?"

When Christopher reached over to console her, she went berserk. Leaping wildly, she smacked him across his face and head repeatedly. With a closed fist she aimlessly threw punches at him until Ty pulled her away.

Eleanor jerked herself out of Ty's grip, breathing heavily. When Ty opened the door, making certain no one was near, she took the opportunity to slip out of her right shoe. She flipped it up in the air and caught it with her left hand. Christopher was wide open to receive several blows from the heel of her shoe before Ty could restrain her. "Calm down," he warned. "They're coming."

The two detectives entering the room reminded Christopher of Abbott and Costello. One was tall, lean and neat. The other one was a short, stubby man with thinning hair who sat down before Christopher and made himself comfortable quickly.

"So tell us what happened," said the short one.

Christopher cleared his throat and dragged his gaze from one person in the room to the other as he spoke. When he finished, the questions came at him relentlessly.

"What were you doing outside of the school building at that time? How long have you been a member of the Dark Shadows? Do you own a gun? Who else is involved? Do you sell drugs?"

Moments later, a court-appointed attorney entered the room. Mr. Diggins was a scrawny-looking man wearing wire-rimmed glasses. His soiled suit looked like it had seen better days and was one size too small for him. "I'd like to confer with my client," he told the detectives. Quickly and impatiently, his words fell out, "What happened here?"

Rehashing the story forced Christopher to relive the incident all over again. Mr. Diggins never took a note, and the expression on his face displayed his boredom. "I suggest you plead out," he said as casually as one would say 'pass the salt.' "You'll probably get two years."

"But I didn't do anything," declared Christopher.

Mr. Diggins interrupted. "If your fingerprints are on the gun, it's as good as yours. That's a mandatory three years. Plus, you can get—"

"But how do I prove the gun doesn't belong to me?"

He sighed wearily, "Uh, trace the serial number, track the history. And hope that it wasn't involved in any other crimes. Then you could be facing more charges." He didn't show a hint of confidence in Christopher's innocence.

"Then I'll just have to prove it." Christopher was adamant.

"How do you suppose that?" Diggins asked, addressing the question to Mrs. Murphy and Ty.

"Well after your investigation is complete, the findings will speak for him, right?" asked his mother.

"Ma'am, we're talking possession of a weapon and manslaughter in the second degree. I'm only a public defender . . . with thirty more cases far more severe than this on my plate. My office doesn't have the time or the money for an investigation of this kind. You might want to consider a private attorney."

Christopher, his mother and Ty exchanged glances.

"What do they charge for something like this?" Mrs. Murphy asked.

"Depends. Fifteen . . . maybe twenty thousand dollars."

A surprised gasp jumped out of Mrs. Murphy and the room went dead silent.

"That's why I say take a plea. With good behavior he could be out in two, maybe two and a half years."

"I'm not pleading out! . . . I'm not pleading out! . . . I'm not pleading . . ."

✛ ✛ ✛

The white lights cast a hazy shadow over the ten-by-ten-foot holding pen where Christopher was escorted while waiting to be processed. A quiet hush came over the room as he entered; the overpowering stench of feces and urine with dried blood stains on the wall making him feel more like puking than running. He took a quick count of five as the bars slammed shut, careful not to look any one of them in the eye. In disbelief, his eyes were drawn to the dirty toilet— stuffed with paper and uneaten food—in full view. The plumbing was obviously out of service. There was no expectation of fine accommodations in jail, but toxic conditions—come on! Inhaling noxious gas, Christopher found an empty spot on the wooden bench and reached for a newspaper he found amongst the clutter on the cracked floor.

The two white boys huddled in the corner had the whole "hood" culture mimicked to a tee: lingo, gestures, and syntax. One of them was troubled, Christopher could tell, but the other one talked nonsense.

"That went down in Spartford two years ago," he was saying, biting his fingernails. He looked like he was thirty, but he was only eighteen. "Ay, I neva seen a dude this big before, for real. He was about seven-nine, yo. Had to be about five hundred pounds, and strong. He would go into these fits, right. And when the guards tried to restrain him, he'd start slammin' the guards around like they was toys."

The other one, who appeared pensive and scared, forced a laugh.

"And I remember this other dude, right—"

He was soon drowned out by the crooning of a short, pudgy, African American with white patches on his brown face. His baritone voice dipped and swayed as he sang an R&B classic. Locked in his own world of trouble, the melodic sound drifted easily out of his soul-filled reservoir. The song sounded strangely eerie and haunting in this chamber of horrors, but something about it gave Christopher the first bit of hope he had felt since he arrived.

Christopher read the newspaper from cover to cover—news, sports, weather, home and garden, business, op-ed, corrections—everything. Soon dinner arrived, which consisted of a stale sandwich wrapped in wax paper. When Christopher opened it there were two slices of cheese inside, hard and discolored at the edges, and the mayonnaise looked yellow. He closed it back up, feeling a sudden loss of appetite.

"You don' wannit?" asked the young man who had been singing. He looked at it as if it were a savory filet mignon.

"Nah, I want to get out of here is what I want."

A different officer magically appeared in front of the cell. He directed Christopher down the corridor to a central area.

A short, pale-white, uniformed officer wearing square black-framed glasses took over. The badge around his neck sat on top of his protruding stomach. "Stand up against the wall, look straight ahead."

"What's this for?" Christopher said. "I'm not a criminal."

The man didn't as much as flinch in response. He was holding a lit cigarette in the right corner of his mouth and preparing the camera.

"But I'm innocent," Christopher pleaded.

"Doesn't matter, you were arrested," he said without an ounce of emotion.

"Why you gotta take my picture? I already told them what happened."

The cigarette bobbed up and down as he squinted his eyes to look through the camera. He took a long drag of the cigarette and the smoke coming out of his mouth resembled thick clouds. "Procedure," he said. "If it's a mistake, these pictures don't mean a thing. They'll seal your records. Look right here into the camera."

Christopher was one for taking pictures, not having them taken, and he hated the thought of a mug shot.

"Now turn to the right," the officer instructed.

He had fingerprinting to look forward to next.

Back in the holding pen, Christopher looked at the six occupants who were anxiously awaiting their fates. One sat on the toilet taking care of his business.

The tall, dark inmate, who looked older than his age, nodded a friendly gesture toward Christopher.

The talkative one walked in circles, jerking his neck and darting his index finger aimlessly, while reciting rap lyrics. He had a lot of acne, big eyes, and thick lips. His hair was a collaboration of loosened braids that had not been combed out. The dingy elastic band around his underwear showed as he turned around.

"My man, what they tryin' to get you for?" he asked Christopher.

"Nothing. I was just defending myself."

"With what?"

"My hands."

"Then how you got here?"

"The other guy had a gun."

"Yo, that happened to me one time," he said and spun his body around in a circle and threw punches in the air. The coincidence excited him. "Check it, right. I was out one night liftin' me up a ride, yo, 'cause I had somethin' to do, know what I'm sayin'. Next thing I know this dude came out of nowhere and hit me across my head with the back of his piece. I thought I was hit yo, so I tried to slash him but he got out of my way. Gun fell out of his hand. I picked it up and tried to squeeze it. Wasn't even no bullets in there. Yo, the cops rolled up, took me to jail."

"What are you in here for now?" Christopher asked.

He grunted, laughed nervously, and then said, "I needed a ride."

"For what?"

"I had to handle my business. Somethin' I needed to do." Remembering the ordeal, he snapped his finger hard like he had just missed an opportunity. "In less than sixty seconds I had that ignition hummin', yo. They chased me for like . . . five miles. I had the pedal to the floor yo; I was smokin' 'em! 'Bout twenty cars started chasin' me and I was doin' one-twenty. I smashed into cars, ran up on sidewalks. All I could see was straight ahead."

Listening to his story gave Christopher the chills as he envisioned the scene. Any one of his family members could have been victims of an unnecessary tragedy. He had everyone's attention now.

"How'd they catch you?" one of the white boys asked.

Reliving the excitement, he threw up his fists and began to pace in a circle. "Yo, I was ready to go out in a blaze 'cause I knew if they got me this time, it was gonna be a long time before I hit the streets. I wasn't goin' there, man. I saw them blocking me way up ahead, but I was going too fast to turn anywhere. I was ready to drive that Lexus right into them but my reflex slowed me down. My head said do it, but my reflexes hit the brakes. I was still doing ninety when I turned the corner. That car did a 360 three times, yo, and that's all I remember."

"What happened after that?" Christopher asked.

"I was in the hospital for three months. Broke seventeen bones, my right shoulder, my wrists. Both my legs was messed up. They holdin' me here now so I can go see the judge. I'm pleading out to fifteen."

They all exchanged glances in disbelief. Christopher did a double take when his eyes fell upon the young man flushing the toilet. His profile looked familiar but he couldn't place him. Finally, he looked toward Christopher and their eyes locked. He could never forget that smug look and that lazy eye. Of all the places to meet an Eastern Thug.

The stench of his elimination overpowered the small room. Christopher was beginning to feel nauseous and felt as though he could taste it in his mouth.

"Dag, man! What crawled up inside you and died?" asked the talkative one.

Embarrassed, he said, "Aay, I couldn't help it. Had to come out somewhere."

Up close, the Thug looked malnourished. He had an ashy darkness, a wandering eye and yellow buckteeth. It was obvious that he had never received any dental care.

Christopher fixed his stare on the Thug until it burned him. The sudden gleam in his eye gave him away. "Remember me?"

"I'm supposed to?"

"As many times as you chased me, yeah."

"Think you got the wrong man."

"No, I don't."

The young man became nervous as Christopher inched toward him. He darted his eyes suspiciously at everyone as they watched the exchange.

"Where you from?"

"Bedville."

"Where in Bedville?"

" Georgia Avenue."

"Who you live with?"

"Why you wanna know?"

"Georgia Avenue? That's where that welfare hotel is. You live there?"

"No!"

"So where do you live?" Christopher asked again, only to appease him. He knew he was lying.

"O-o-n the other side of Georgia."

"That was you chasing me?"

"Nah."

Christopher inched even closer, backing him into a corner. "You got beef with me, I don't even know you." He removed his shirt and without warning he drove his fist into the wall above his head, scaring him. "I'm here now. You got me all to yourself."

"Showtime, yo!" the talkative one said. Again, he became excited.

The other young men crowded around, anticipating the action.

The Thug inched up on his feet but somehow lost his balance and fell back on the bench. Christopher then lunged forward and went straight for his neck with both hands, gripping it with all his strength. As the Thug fell helpless at the ominous undertaking, his face began to transform. Suddenly, before his very eyes, his father's face stared up at him, clenched between his hands. Christopher dropped him as if he were a red-hot coal and stared. His father's face disappeared and the young man's face returned. Then he backed away further and further . . .

Eleanor Murphy and Ty exchanged few words during the ride to the precinct. Without James Murphy, she feared for her sons' futures, her most valuable and precious possessions. Now, one of them was caught between the clutches of an unkind judicial system. "Young black boys— easy prey," her husband always told her. It was a place she had prayed to God not to ever have to visit. She closed her eyes, reliving old times, trials and triumphs, good days and better ones. "Hold on to your faith, Ellie," she could hear James saying, "Hold on to your faith." She unfolded the message she'd received from Coach Lappatina and called him to acknowledge his concerns.

The judge presiding over the arraignment was a large white man with a fat nose and bulging eyes. He was bald on top with a mass of wild, gray hair hanging long on the sides.

"Your honor," said the lawyer, ripping into his presentation of the facts. "My client is a sixteen-year-old junior at Telham Park High School. He's a B-average student, a member of the track team and has no priors."

"Ah huh," replied the judge, swiveling his chair from side to side.

"He was defending his friend against a known gang member who was being beaten outside the school . . . and now on critical watch at Yorkstown Memorial Hospital. My client has never been in trouble before. His actions were purely in self-defense and in defense of his friend. The police found a weapon, uh . . . that did not belong to him. Your honor, my client is ready to take a plea."

The judge rambled on and on with some legal mumbo-jumbo. There was only one sentence Christopher heard. "You will serve three years in a correctional facility." He banged his gavel three times and said, "Next."

✥ ✥ ✥

In spite of the noise, he could still hear the rattling of the chains that bound his feet. On the second tier, shouts and obscenities from inmates followed him down the corridor as officers escorted him. Darkness moved into Christopher's mind as he looked out at the deathly hue of their hopeless faces.

His new home was an eight-by-eight-foot cell. A pull string operated the light bulb that lit the space. A small cot with a three-inch mattress would serve as his bed. The rusty sink next to it looked like it had not seen a flow of water in some time. Underneath it was a sanitary bucket that was to be used as the toilet with half a roll of tissue paper next to it. And there was nothing to read anywhere.

Early each morning, Christopher was awakened to eat, shower, and empty his bucket. By 6:00 a.m. he was already at work. For five cents an hour he performed several back-breaking duties. He dug up acres and acres of soil for a landscaping group. He transported thousands of pounds of solid bricks and limestone for a city construction company. He put down black tar for miles and miles of interstate highways.

When he wasn't working, he devoured books like a famished man—on any subject, any category. His library time was limited to only thirty minutes a day with a puny collection of history books. So he began making up his own stories. Soon, the monotony and routine began to wear on him. He felt as if he were dying a slow death. At night he'd

sit up grasping the metal bars to see the shadows of the
men in authority moving throughout the corridors. He'd
run his hands from the top of the bars down to the floor.
He could smell the metal that rubbed off on his hands, and
after a while he felt like he could taste it. Falling deeper into
depression, he was slowly dying . . . slowly . . . dying . . .

WAKING UP from his forty-seven minute tormented slumber; Christopher was startled by the unfamiliar surroundings. The taste of burnt metal in his mouth disturbed him, and those thumping palpitations returned. While stretching his sore hand and rummaging through the day's horrible events, something moved inside him. Christopher sprang to his feet and paced around the table. Remembering suddenly that interrogation rooms have two-way mirrors, he summoned up a proud, respectful demeanor.

Another hour passed, leaving Christopher to recall the terrifying details of his dream. Envisioning himself on the side of the road in prison apparel sent spasms shooting throughout his body. He thought of Princess. Would she visit him? Then he thought of his mother and Joshua. A criminal record at sixteen? Forever checking "yes" to the question: "Have you ever been arrested?" But I know it can be expunged. It has to be. I didn't do anything, he chanted over and over again. The robust sound of Gilroy's trumpet shifting melodically and harmonically, spewing emotional jazz played loudly in his head. Who would look after Pop-Pop?

Ty held the door for Eleanor Murphy as she entered the precinct. He was, unfortunately, all too familiar with the hostile environment that reeked of condemnation. "We're looking for Christopher Murphy," he told the officer at the desk. "He's been detained."

"Step this way, please."

"I want to see my son," Mrs. Murphy told the officer. "When can I—"

"Shouldn't be long."

Ty led her to the waiting area as Mrs. Murphy questioned his need for representation.

MIRED IN critical self-examination, Christopher continued thinking. He didn't hate the Eastern Thugs, but he despised the warfare they inflicted on others. This day would have never happened if it weren't for them. Strangely, he grew sympathetic to their plight: poor and uneducated; no purpose in their lives; no guidance to direct them. They were powerless pawns seeking some kind of recognition.

WHEN THE door opened, Christopher felt a streak of panic. Mrs. Murphy and Ty appeared larger than usual as they entered the room. Accompanying them was a well-dressed white man. There was tension in his mother's proud, beautiful face and he sensed her fear. Christopher wanted to grab her and bury his head in her warm bosom like he did as a child.

"You alright, Son?"

"Yes."

Ty embraced him with assurance, looking more concerned than judgmental.

"Bill Harrington, attorney," greeted the white man, extending his hand to Christopher. He was dressed in a navy-blue suit. "I'll be representing you."

The cost of his services was Christopher's initial thoughts as they were being seated. The gentleman was no public defender, he could tell.

"Want to tell us what brought you here today?" Harrington asked, removing a legal pad from his briefcase.

Christopher truthfully explained the day's events as Harrington took copious notes.

Then a barrage of questions came. "How old are you? Do you have any criminal history? What's your grade point average? Perform in extracurricular activities? Do you work?"

A detective soon entered the room addressing everyone. He was a tough-looking brown-haired white man, very tall, in his fifties. Wearing a blue oxford shirt and beige khakis, his gun and holster were openly displayed.

"Christopher's been detained because of an altercation that occurred outside his school today," he began. "An automatic .22 caliber was found on the scene. Possession of a weapon in New York City is a crime. Here's the issue: Who does the gun belong to?"

"It doesn't belong to my client," replied the attorney. Now in his full professional mode, his presence swelled in the room.

"The other young man claims it does."

"How could this kid pull a weapon on Christopher here, *if* it belonged to him? Doesn't make any sense. Anyway, we've got ten witnesses who can corroborate the truth."

"That kid said it belonged to you," the detective countered.

"No, it doesn't!" denied Christopher. "I was trying to help Deshon. They were gonna kill him!"

"And the boy's the son of a correction officer," Ty added.

"The fingerprints will tell us the truth, right?" stated Harrington.

Mrs. Murphy looked confused. "And how long is that going—"

"In that case, you have nothing to charge my client with. He's free to go."

"Not so fast," said the detective, halting the dismissal. "There's an assault charge pending."

"From someone with a criminal record from here to Baltimore? C'mon, don't waste the court's time. This kid is clean."

"What's his affiliation with the gangs?"

"My client doesn't have any affiliation with them." Harrington spoke sternly.

"The other young man said you're with the Shadows."

"That's not true, Sir. They've been after me for a while."

Ty nodded, confirming Christopher's statement.

"Why is that?" the detective asked.

"Trying to recruit me. They chased me down what, two or three times already. I had to fight 'em off."

A surprise gasp leaped from his mother. "Why would they want—"

"You ever owned a gun?" The detective's face was tight as he fixed his gaze onto Christopher's. He was trying to get a read on the truth of his story.

"No!"

"How would you explain your fingerprints on the gun?"

"My client hasn't been fingerprinted," Mr. Harrington boldly interjected. "So you don't know that."

The detective's taut expression slid into a sly grin. "I meant to say *if* your prints were found on the weapon." And then he took a deep breath, knocked on the wooden table, and excused himself.

"Is he going to be fingerprinted?" Mrs. Murphy asked the attorney.

"They haven't charged him with anything yet, so—"

"Lord, have mercy."

"What about the assault charge on the other kid?" Ty asked.

"If they took that seriously, they would have charged Christopher already. And we could counter that same charge. The kid assaulted Christopher. But he's already been booked in juvenile detention." Mr. Harrington deposited his notepad and pen in his briefcase. "There is still the possibility, however—"

The detective returned to the room with a cup of coffee in his hand, interrupting Mr. Harrington. The room fell silent. "The test results on the fingerprints will take a minute. If we find anything, we'll be calling you back. Until then, sit tight."

"Very well then," Mr. Harrington said. "We're free to leave."

IT WAS SURREAL. Christopher walked out of the precinct and into the quiet of night in a daze.

"Why didn't you tell me what was going on, with those boys coming after you?" asked Mrs. Murphy, a sense of relief apparent in her voice, holding onto her son's arm.

"I didn't want to worry you with all that, Ma."

"Worry me? Instead, you'd rather shock me to death with a call telling me you're being held at the police precinct . . . or that something worse has happened to you? Don't ever do this to me again, Son. Your problems are my problems, and I can't help you if you don't talk to me."

"That's right," Ty agreed, opening the doors of the vehicle. "We're both here for you."

"I knew you were distracted for a reason. When we get home, we've got some serious talking to do."

Christopher remained quiet for the duration of the ride home.

eleven

Navigating through a maze of terrifying dreams, Christopher was awakened abruptly by what he thought to be the touch of a hand. Spooked, he scanned the room wildly until its familiarity calmed him. Sitting up, he ran his hand along the edge of the mattress, grateful for the privilege of being in his own comfortable bed. *Thank you, God!*

Christopher looked over at Joshua, who was not yet awake, the thin rays of sun beaming generously upon him. He resembled their father, even in his sleep. Massaging his swollen hand, Christopher began recalling some of his father's teachings. *Don't ride the tide of mediocrity or follow the masses, Son. You don't want someone controlling your thinking, your time, and your money. Work with the gifts GOD gave you...because He gave them to you for a purpose. Find your way with it, you'll find freedom, and do it now... because time is short."* He clung to the words of his new higher consciousness, understanding its relevance for the first time.

Lingering in his thoughts, Christopher remembered his father spending weekday evenings reading and preparing for the commercial cleaning business he had planned to start. Sometimes he only worked ten minutes before he would fall asleep. The next morning he'd say, 'I'm ten minutes closer to my dream.' He'd give Christopher a task to complete like putting together a two hundred-piece puzzle, or reading a voluminous history book that would take him weeks to finish. Then he would say, "Work a little bit toward it every day and before you know it, the job is complete."

Joshua was up and showered now. Dressing in the same way Christopher did, he put on his pants first and then put the belt through the loops, buckled up, and then put on his shirt. Only today, the shirt needed to go inside the pants.

"No, li'l man. When you're gonna wear the shirt inside," he explained, unbuckling his belt. "You put your shirt in first and then buckle up."

Soon Christopher had them both dressed with the beds made, and Joshua's lunch prepared. He moved quietly the whole time, hoping his mother didn't awaken. He wanted her to sleep as long as she needed to.

Aim: Capital Punishment:
Are You For or Against It?

Attendance was good in American Government for a Tuesday. The issue of capital punishment had been assigned for the week's current events discussion, following a recent governor's decision to pardon an innocent man in Chicago.

Jordan walked into class late, mouthing the notes on the board. "I'ma sit with you," he said, dropping a stack of books on the desk next to Christopher. "This is one of our subjects right here."

One student opened the discussion of women on death row with a story he'd found on a malicious murder carried out by a female. He read portions of the article out loud.

"Okay, there's no doubt she's guilty, but she's a woman. Does it make any difference?" Mr. Feldman asked the class. The only white teacher in Telham Park High School wore dreads with his khakis and oxford shirts.

"It shouldn't," answered a young man in the back. "Guilty is guilty, so she deserves the same punishment."

"Yeah, but I don't see a woman going out like that," another male student countered. "I don't believe in it anyway."

"Alright, we know the obvious reasons that people favor the death penalty," said the blue-eyed, dirty blond, middle-aged activist that some students referred to as 'the white Rasta.' "But what are the arguments against it?"

"Innocent people might get killed," replied Triana, a heavy-set, fair-skinned girl with freckles.

Kila raised her hand. "It's a violation of the fifth commandment. 'Thou shall not kill.'" She was a Nigerian girl who was a member of the debate team.

"You might not feel the same way if it were your brother," David, a boy from Haiti, argued. He hardly ever spoke out in class.

"But the system is biased," Christopher stated flatly.

"Come again, Chris," Mr. Feldman said. "And speak louder."

"The system is biased. Minorities and poor people don't get the same opportunities."

"Be more specific," Mr. Feldman pressed. He loved to challenge Christopher.

"Okay, say you're Hispanic, you're Black or any other so-called minority. Somebody picks you out of a lineup—mistakenly, 'cause brothers of color are always profiled. You gotta get a court-appointed lawyer to defend you 'cause you can't afford one. I mean how many people got thousands of dollars lying around waiting to throw it in the hands of some greedy lawyer? So you got to settle for the attorney the court gives you, and they're usually like . . . right out of law school or," Christopher turned toward the class and continued, "stressed to the max. They don't have extra money for like . . . DNA testing, researchers or private investigators. Then they got twenty, thirty other cases just like yours, so how much attention do you think the defendant is going to get?"

"Are you saying they're not gonna get a fair trial?" asked Mr. Feldman.

"Not like a person with money would."

"People with money don't go to jail," agreed Robert Lee, an Asian boy.

"Not necessarily," Craig objected. He was a master in the lyrical freestyle competition. No one could touch him rapping. "Look at Nye from L.A. He's Black. He's rich. He's doing time."

"Yeah, but we're not talkin' about somebody who's guilty as sin, a parole violator and all that," argued Christopher. "He just got a little too big for his britches. That's different. But what I'm saying is that a little money and some fame helps. I mean, there's never gonna be any mistaken identity with Shaquille."

"Huh," Mr. Feldman grunted approvingly.

"To find a person guilty with money, his fingerprints would have to be around the victim's neck with fifty eyewitnesses," Christopher continued. "And then he still might get off with a lesser charge 'cause he can afford the defense. Lawyer can claim he's crazy or something, and if he pays off all the witnesses, he can walk."

"Are you saying the system works in favor of the rich?" Mr. Feldman asked. "Because that would negate your premise that justice turns a blind eye to minorities because some of them are rich."

Christopher thought for a moment as he doodled with his pen. "Yeah, that's what I'm saying. The blind eye can suddenly see when that minority has money; otherwise, they're hit."

Mr. Feldman cocked a bushy brow inquiringly and looked around the room, inviting others' participation.

"But you got all these other issues too," Christopher added.

"Such as?"

"You got these housewife jurors and these other people who don't have a clue about the law. They couldn't care less about a trial and jury duty. They just want to go home. Then you got these overzealous prosecutors—I learned that on this show I watch called *Prejudiced Judges*. Yo, the system is too corrupt to have the death penalty. People are dyin' for nothing and the majority of them look like me. And if you look at the number of men on death row, how can they be so high when we make up only thirteen-and-a-half percent of the population? That would mean most of us are criminals, and that's not true."

Mr. Feldman admired Christopher's confident and knowledgeable delivery. He positioned him to defend his every statement. Others joined in, and soon Christopher's contribution had turned the mundane assignment into a spirited discussion.

"You workin' them hard," Jordan said to Christopher. "You got the mind, a voice, the patience— Why you stallin'? Telham Intelligence can use you right now!"

"What y'all workin' on?"

Surprised, Jordan did a double take. "Affirmative Action," he replied quickly. "What do you know about it?"

"Access, man. Without it, discrimination prevails. It's necessary to keep the people in the loop. Otherwise, we would never get a break, 'cause power and privilege does not concede."

"The Bakke case argues its reverse discrimination," Jordan challenged.

"That's bull! And I'ma tell you why . . . not right now, though. I'll hit you wid it later when we can talk."

"*Obedience is better than sacrifice,*" pondered Christopher, reading the pamphlet handed to him by Nikita Jones between classes. Happy for every moment, he made time to listen to the 'Students for Christ' member and considered her invitation to attend this evening's bible study.

"All the good you do in this world means nothing for your personal salvation."

Good deeds don't make up for bad living. That's what Christopher heard her say and nodded in agreement. "I won't promise you I'll be there tonight, but I'm gonna read this."

"Slow down, Lightning, where you going?" asked Coach Lappatina, gripping him from the back.

"Coach, whassup?"

"What's going on, everything okay?"

"Yeah, what about you?" Christopher asked, observing his red, tired eyes.

"I was up late last night. Had to call on a favor from an old partner. Then, this attorney friend of mine, a guy I went to school with, made a visit to a precinct for me. Somebody I knew was in trouble and needed some help. We all got together after that and—"

Christopher stopped in his tracks, shocked.

"Harrington?"

Coach Lappatina nodded slowly, looking off into nowhere in particular.

"You did that for me?"

"That's between us," he murmured huskily, leaning toward him. "Figure somebody like you deserves a second chance." Even amid all the noise in the hallway, Christopher could hear every word the coach said. "You could have been killed yesterday."

"I know," Christopher admitted, ashamed. For two years the coach had hounded him, pleaded with him to join the track team, and he had treated the opportunity like it would always be there. Like he would always be sixteen and fast as lightning. "That was an experience, Coach, and you don't ever have to—"

"I know it was, but you're smart. You'll learn from it, right?"

"Oh, definitely." Reaching the end of the corridor, Christopher pushed open the exit door where he knew they'd part and asked, "What do I owe you?"

"You don't owe me anything. But you think you might ah … be interested in coming out to practice tomorrow?"

"Who, me?"

"Yeah, you."

With a sly grin, Christopher turned away, then turned toward the coach and said, "Before sun-up or what?"

YORKSTOWN MEMORIAL Hospital had been an unpleasant memory for Christopher since his father fell ill. He glanced up at the old brick building. No portion of its solid structure had changed in years. The windows were small yet prominent. Like little beady eyes, they watched you— waiting to capture you at any moment of vulnerability and pull you in.

Christopher brought Ty along with him to visit Deshon, who had been there for several days. The visit was brief and few words were spoken. He and Ty walked in silence as they exited the fourth floor. Once outside, Christopher shook off the unnerving sight of his friend, now appearing like a dream. The sky hung low with a dreariness that was as heavy as Christopher's thoughts as he and Ty crossed the street.

"Could have been you up there," Ty said, driving off.

"Yeah, I know. Didn't see it coming."

"It was inevitable, I told you."

"You saw his face? Eyes swollen and mouth looking deformed. I didn't recognize him at first. Couldn't believe they busted his ribs."

"It's not as bad as it looks. Would've been worse if you hadn't helped him. We might've only been attending two funerals instead of one." Ty was being sarcastic.

"But if I didn't help him, they would have finished Deshon."

"And since you did, they could have killed you both."

Christopher watched the people on the street going about their lives. "I don't know, man. Something just . . . but I couldn't just stand there and let him—"

"That's why you had no business being there," Ty chided.

"But it was like . . . something came over me. I knew he was in trouble. I could feel it."

Ty looked over at Christopher sternly. "Oh, so you cut out of school and hit the streets so you could go save your friend. The same friend who wants you to get down with the Thugs . . . yeah, okay. And sittin' in a hospital bed, he's still talking revenge."

"He didn't say anything about—"

"Not out of his mouth," Ty clarified. "But I see it all in 'im. For some people that's all there is to them . . . and payback begets another payback. Friend? Your friend is your father, your mother, and the person sitting next to you."

The truth was striking, simple, yet difficult to swallow. Christopher didn't attempt to reply.

"Let me tell you something. Don't ever confront a situation unless you're ready to die for it, understand me? What if that gun had fired? It might have killed you. What kind of life would have been left for your mother and brother?"

"It's true."

"It's good you were able to handle yourself like that," Ty commended. "When a man points a gun at you, and you never had any experience with a weapon, it can rattle you."

Up ahead two fire trucks were returning to their station. Two firefighters, one Black, the other white, jumped out and stalled the traffic until the vehicles were safely inside. They had always looked so strong and mighty to Christopher when he was child—wearing those big hats and boots. Today he realized they were just ordinary men on a gigantic mission, one step ahead of their own fear.

"I had a gun, Ty." Courageously and impulsively, the words flew out of his mouth.

"Where did you get it from?" There was no reaction in Ty's monotone voice.

"Bought it from this white dude."

"You talking about Frankie? Short dude, got like a slanted left eye?"

Christopher turned toward Ty, surprised. "You know him?"

"Yeah, I know him," Ty grunted.

"He hooked us up," Christopher said. "Showed us how to work 'em and everything."

Again Ty grunted and cocked his head to one side. "So you're walking around the streets carrying a gun, riding in my vehicle, taking it home to your mother's house? Do you know what kind of position you could have put us in?" His tone now was blunt and unsympathetic, nearly intolerant.

"I didn't know what else to do. I was tired of runnin' and taking their hits, man. Looking over my shoulder every minute, I felt stupid."

Ty digested Christopher's reasoning, empathizing with his plight. He saw aspects of himself at the same age: aimless ambition, unlimited energy, angry, confused and misunderstood.

"You had other options," he stated lightly. "Look, I know it's not easy—"

"It's not, Ty, and sometimes I feel like . . . this is crazy. I hang with my friends, but I'm not gettin' nothin' from them. Then in school—"

"So what do you want?"

"I'm not sure. You know I like working and making money, but . . . what's my purpose? What am I supposed to be doin'?"

Ty turned into the parking lot of the Mini Paradise Café. They sat and enjoyed a late lunch with café lattes and talked as men with dreams and aspirations do.

By the time they walked out, laughing like boys, the parking lot was practically empty. A shy sun peered through the clouds. Christopher, having bonded closely with Ty, wondered about his presence.

"How come you're here, Ty?"

"What do you . . . I don't understand the question?"

"Like why are you here . . . with me? In my life right now?"

"I don't know. Some people believe God gives you what you need. Or He sometimes replaces a loved one with someone else." Ty released the locks with his remote key but neither of them reached for the door. They looked at each other across the roof of the Navigator and continued.

"So you don't think this is a coincidence?"

"I don't believe in coincidences. Like I said, sometimes we're given just what we need. We don't always know it at the time, but when you look back . . . you'll find it was all a part of God's unfathomable plan."

"But do you understand what I'm sayin'? Why you, Ty?"

"You mean as opposed to it being any Joe, William or Thomas?"

"Yeah."

"Now you're getting philosophical on me? I don't know. Why's the sky blue and the grass green? These things," Ty held up his hands, his palms facing Christopher. "Why are they hands?" His thick fingers reminded him so much of his father's. "You're looking for explanations to the universe. I don't have them."

"So you're sayin' it's like destiny?"

"Well, think about it. I'm here because your father chose me. I needed a life preserver and he threw me one. Or, maybe I chose him. Ever thought about that? I needed somebody in my life, and at the same time he was preparing me to be here for you."

"But why you?"

"I already told you." Ty smiled, watching a van full of people pull in. "Ay, maybe to be the godfather to your children."

A partial smile drew up around Christopher's questioning eyes as they entered the vehicle. "What do you mean?"

Ty paused and grunted. "I'ma take you to my house. I got something to show you."

TY'S BROWNSTONE was clean and unique, with its lofty walls, high ceilings and spaciousness, but most impressive was the serenity that enveloped Christopher upon entering. The living room was sparsely decorated with fine antiques, and earth-tone furnishings accented with a New Zealand wool rug on the polished wood floor.

Christopher sank into an armchair next to the fireplace, cushioned by a plush, decorative pillow. An oil painting of a country landscape was set above the mantel between two sets of long brass candleholders. He wondered what part of the world the painting depicted.

Ty returned to Christopher carrying a small safe deposit box and handed him an envelope from inside.

When Christopher removed its contents his eyes grew large. "This looks like . . . a copy of— "

"A check," Ty confirmed.

"For one hundred thousand dollars?"

"Yes."

"Where did you get this from?"

"Your father."

"My father?" Christopher frowned in bewilderment.

Ty looked at him and crossed his legs just like Mr. Murphy used to do when he wanted to talk seriously. "When your father died I was still locked up. You know he used to come and visit me all the time, right?"

"Yeah."

"I remember that day when they called me to the social worker's office. My heart dropped. I knew something had happened, but I thought it was my mother or another member of my family." Ty stared at the wall and into the past. "Anyway, this letter came to my sister's house a few months later and she brought it to me. It was from an insurance company."

Christopher sat up straight, displaying his heightened interest.

"He took out a life insurance policy on himself and made me the beneficiary. Understand?"

Christopher slowly nodded. "I understand, but . . ." His eyes wandered over the room and then returned to Ty. For a fleeting moment, and in the way the setting sun cast a shadow on one side of his face, he saw his father. It was as if there were three men in the room. The reason behind James Murphy's action became a question to both of them.

"You know, uh . . . we always talked about starting a business together. At the time it was just talk to me, but he was serious. I think he was a man ahead of his time. So he took out an insurance policy, I guess," Ty shrugged. "Maybe he was just being cautious, just in case anything ever happened to him. I mean, I don't think he had any idea that he was gonna die, but then again, maybe he did. To tell you the truth I never understood why he left this for me. Was it intended for me to get back on my feet just in case he wasn't around, start the business, or to look out for you and Joshua—I don't know."

"You always said you would send me to college," Christopher recalled.

"I was going to do that anyway."

"So what did you spend it on?"

"Never touched it. It's sittin' in the bank. Even when I bought all of this, I never used it."

"Why?"

Ty leaned forward and rubbed his hands together. " 'Cause that's the greatest demonstration of faith that anyone has ever had in me. And I have to do right by this . . . do something significant with it. I call it the seed."

Again the question of James Murphy's intentions loomed large in the air, but neither one spoke about it. Ty reached for the copy of the check. "Don't tell anybody about this, not even your mother, understand?"

"Yes."

Something touched Christopher's inner sanctum of emotions staring into Ty's face. Despite a plethora of questions flooding his mind, he felt in that instant that their relationship had grown even deeper. In Ty's presence he felt protected, and a duty to succeed as if he were part of something noble and purposeful. Christopher left Ty's home that evening a different man than when he came.

"On Your Mark . . . Get Set . . ."

The gun cracked when it fired. In his first indoor competition of the *Highland Relay Classics*, running the fifty-five meter race, Christopher dashed out ahead of seven competitors. The audience exploded with a wild charge that electrified him, spurring him to reach the finishing line—first. In his mind and his periphery Christopher saw no competition; his feet abiding by his will. And for the briefest of moments, the noiseless bed of cold rubber began elevating, rising to a plateau of which champions reached, where there was no fear, and no failure.

In the distance, desperate cries of victory shouted out. Friends and families were cheering furiously, vicariously applauding their own hopes and dreams. The hollow screams for those who would never be, or never win, came at him swift and loud. For them, he ran even faster, slicing the wind and denying any lurking defeat.

Owning the moment, Christopher crossed the finishing line in record time, parting the zealous crowd like a hot knife through butter, the victory ribbon clinging to his body.

"I love it, baby! You broke a record!" Coach Lappatina charged him, lifting him off his feet. "We're going to the top! Ya heard? We're going to the top!" Ecstatic, the coach's beet-red face faded as the crowd surged upon him. Arms reached for him and hands pulled at him, reveling in the glory of his decisive win. Christopher felt sobered for the briefest of moments as James Murphy's presence washed over him.

"Coming in first for the fifty-five meter dash and setting a new school record is Christopher Murphy of Telham Park High School," the sports commentator pridefully announced. Another layer of roars ensued.

Christopher looked around and caught a glimpse of the proud faces of his mother and Joshua, who were joined by Pam and Ty. Even his boss, Victor, had made time to come to see him run and was cheering wildly for his win. The 'Round the World' ride that his father used to take him on revisited him. Holding him by the wrists, he would swing him around and around and when he stopped, the world was still spinning. It was an exhilarating feeling, exactly the way he was feeling right now.

YOUR MAIL has been sent. Christopher clicked OK and spun around in his desk chair, thinking about the work that lies ahead. Although his repertoire of knowledge on the death penalty was adequate, he could get specific names and statistics from the *Freedom Project* to support his thesis against its implementation. He wanted to be well-versed on the issue, now that he was contemplating joining the debate team.

"Dinner's ready," announced his mother. "Y'all come and eat."

"In a minute," Christopher replied, lining up pages of Geometry and Trigonometry problems. He examined the trigonometric ratios and put his notes aside in preparation for Tuesday's quiz.

His track victory inspired him to reorder his priorities and sharpen his focus. Over and over in his mind he relived his triumphant moment—now only a day old. Intoxicated by the thrill of his win, he couldn't wait to share what had happened with Princess. After dinner, Christopher returned to his room and saw that Princess was online.

Instant Message:

FlightRisk: I couldn't believe it, Buttah. I just took off.

SmoovAsButtah: I want to see the video!

FlightRisk: What! Everybody had their video cams and it was televised on cable.

SmoovAsButtah: Were you scared?

FlightRisk: I wouldn't say scared, but it seemed like the whole world was watching. And all that attention is not really about me.

SmoovAsButtah: Maybe not, but running is. It's what everybody's been telling you. You were the only one that didn't see it, but I am sooooooo happy.

FlightRisk: I still don't believe it.

SmoovAsButtah: Well I do. Why didn't you tell me you joined the team?

FlightRisk: I don't know. So much was going on and I wasn't sure I was gonna win, so I kept it on the DL.

SmoovAsButtah: That's what you thought. I've got ears all over the place.

FlightRisk: You knew?

SmoovAsButtah: Yep-per.

FlightRisk: Does this mean you knew about everything else, too?

SmoovAsButtah: Almost passed out when I heard about it.

FlightRisk: That wasn't supposed to happen, Buttah. Wrong place, wrong time. I'm just thankful it wasn't worse.

SmoovAsButtah: I knew something was brewing . . . I could feel it. I know your mom was miffed!

FlightRisk: That's an understatement, but she's good now. That look on her face . . . I don't ever want to see it again.

SmoovAsButtah: Coming to your senses. That's great! How's Joshua doing?

FlightRisk: He's good. Still my shadow. How are you making out on the ancient civilization project?

SmoovAsButtah: Pretty good. I'm doing the history of the pyramids.

FlightRisk: Read the book called *Ancient Pyramids*. It will give you a lot of info. And before I forget, I'm giving some thought to this debate team. Jordan is trying to turn me on. What do you think?

SmoovAsButtah: Is that a question?

FlightRisk: Between you and me, I'm really feeling it. My father and I use to debate all the time. I thought we were just talking. We discussed Martin and Malcolm, Capitalism vs. Socialism, and I was just a kid.

SmoovAsButtah: Then it should be a piece of cake. Just have to organize your time.

FlightRisk: You're right. I'm still not sure if I want to put all this pressure on myself.

SmoovAsButtah: Why? You have something else better to do?

FlightRisk: Cut a brother a break. I'm thinking, I'm thinking.

SmoovAsButtah: Think long, you think wrong and you'll talk yourself out of it. JUST DO IT!

FlightRisk: Why can't you be here, Buttah? I get motivated when I'm talking to you.

SmoovAsButtah: Maybe that's why. Can't depend on someone else to motivate you. It has to come from you. Next time you run, I'll be there . . . I hope. Many CONGRATS!!!! I gotta get back to my work. Midterms are coming. Peace.

FlightRisk: Nothing but love.

THE HOUSE phone rang almost five times before Christopher picked it up. After a long and strenuous track practice that afternoon, a two-hour study session, and several phone conversations, he fell asleep early. Though it had been a week since the race, people were still calling to congratulate him and relive the moment.

"Hello."

"Hello. Can I speak to Christopher?"

"Speaking. Who's this?"

"It's me, Maverick."

"Whassup, man? You sound different. Tryin' to disguise your voice or somethin'?"

In Maverick's pause Christopher sensed trouble.

"Bad news, man."

"What happened?"

"They arrested Deshon."

"Don't tell me that . . . for what?"

"Fightin'. He had that piece on 'im, too. Tried to run, but they got 'im."

"No!" Christopher bellowed, springing forward.

As Maverick slid into a recital of details, thoughts of Ty's warnings, his coach's motivational mantras, and his mother's words invaded him. The news brought panic into him, remembering how he narrowly escaped what would have been a major pitfall. In his dark, quiet room, he could hear the echo of his heavy breathing in the receiver, sounding thunderously loud, and he could feel the vibration of his pounding heart. A sudden thrust of gloom set in as he contemplated the grim consequences possibly awaiting Deshon . . . and the phone slipped out of his hand.

"Chris, you there?" Maverick asked. "Yo Chris . . . Chris!"

Christopher slid down the wall, his knees buckling as he hit the floor. He laughed a sorry man's laugh remembering the sound of the gun; the unforgettable flush of victory washing over him.

The starter's gun signaled a new beginning. In my first indoor competition of the Highland Relay Classics, running the fifty-five meter race, I dashed out ahead of seven competitors. The audience exploded with a wild charge that electrified me, spurring my mind to reach the finishing line—first! In my periphery I saw no competition; my feet were like my soldiers, abided by my command. And for the briefest of moments, the noiseless bed of cold rubber began elevating, rising to a plateau of which champions reached, where there was no fear, and no failure. And there I was . . . on the other side of the finishing line.

Why didn't you listen to me, Deshon! Now I know that had to be you, Dad, looking out for me. Who else could be my eyes when I had no vision? My mind when I experienced a temporary lapse of judgment. Who else would order my steps when I was moon walking sideways? Or place people in my life that want to help me. And now that I have ears, I'm gonna do just what you tell me to do. I'm not trying to end up like my best friend and disappoint you and mom. Just watch me.

ABOUT THE AUTHOR

JENNIFER BURTON, a native of New York City, has always been intrigued with multicultural interaction. While teaching in a Brooklyn high school, she became deeply steeped in youth culture, observing their enthusiasm for urban contemporary fiction. Her literary insight, along with her passion for writing, prompted the creation of the Telham Park series. Jennifer resides in New Jersey.